Praise for
The Brooklyn Leprechaun
mystery series

(The Brooklyn Leprechaun is)
"Delightful—full of fun, humor, action and adventure".

Penny Warner
National Bestselling Author,
'How to Host a Killer Party!'
www.pennywarner.com

"If you are a young adult or young at heart, this is a mystery to entertain and inspire".

Dorothy Churchill, Author
'From Mourning to Morning'

"Brooklyn Leprechaun is a great Celtic romp—I want a Mick of my very own!"

Suzanne Johnson, Author
'Royal Street and River Road'

Royal Spirits

A Brooklyn Leprechaun Mystery

Bernadette Crepeau

This is a work of fiction. The events and characters described herein are imaginary and are not intended to refer to specific places or living persons. The opinions expressed in this manuscript are solely the opinions of the author and do not represent the opinions or thoughts of the publisher. The author has represented and warranted full ownership and/or legal right to publish all the materials in this book.

Royal Spirits
Book two of *The Brooklyn Leprechaun mystery series*
All Rights Reserved.
Copyright © 2011 Bernadette Crepeau
ISBN 978-0-615439-19-8
Library of Congress Control Number: 2011900952

PRINTED IN THE UNITED STATES OF AMERICA

This book is dedicated to

My youngest fans
Cade Duarte & Natalie Crepeau

The great men & women serving in
The Armed Forces

The wonderful folks at
The Royal British Legion
Battersea, England

And in loving memory of
Mick and John Regan

Acknowledgments

Without the help and enthusiasm of the following
friends, this book would never have gone to press.
Thank you all so very much!

Carol Bodenhamer, Lynne Borden, Dorothy Churchill,
Susan Cushman, RaeAnne Fox (for all things British),
George Gurney, Ellen Lager, Pat Landers, and Liz Pollock

A special thanks to my daughter,
Bernadette Minshull, for ongoing tech support ☺

I would especially like to thank Diane Stewart for the
beautiful cover art.

Cast of Characters
& Places

Bridget

Born in Brooklyn, N.Y. Inherited land in Ireland where she met her immortal ancestors. She is street smart, but lacks confidence. The Fae set out a few minor challenges for her to build up her courage before she must take down Morrigan, and save the entire Fae race. Her faerie and leprechaun blood helps, but first she must believe in herself and allow her powers to come.

Battersea British Legion

Actual place and wonderful people. Names and descriptions of people are my imagination at work.

Cathcaruth

Holding place for Fae under Morrigan's influence.

Friar Xavier

Friar Francis Xavier is a five hundred year old spirit.

Geraldine,

Faeire, Queen of all Fae, cousin to Morrigan, and Bridget's many times great-grandmother.

Michelle

Born and raised in France. Veterinary assistant to the Queen's prized dogs.

Mary

Bridget's best friend, her mother took in Bridget at the age of twelve after her father died and she was living on the streets of Brooklyn.

Mick aka Lord Howth

A handsome wizard, a distraction to young women, he must shape shift into the guise of a Brittney spaniel to mentor Bridget in all things magic.

Aunt Molly

Bridget's mortal aunt from Dublin, Ireland. Has a wee-bit of magic.

Morrigan- Goddess of War

She wants Fae power to assist her in worldwide destruction. First she needs to take over land in Ireland and all of the Fae to accomplish this. Now she only has control of the Elder Fae, some evil Fae and creatures she has created.

Peter Carins

Bridget's cousin whom she hopes will move to Ireland and take care of the land and keep it safe for her Fae family.

Padraig

Is King of the Leprechauns, husband to
Queen Geraldine and Bridget's many times great-
 grandfather.

Que-tip

Teen faeire with cotton ball hair.

Simon

British secret agent and Mary's boyfriend.

Stan...

Military slang for Afghanistan Pg 121

♣ x ♣

Chapter 1

Meet the Spirit

"Crack on mate! Get a bloody move on! Shut those yappers up, we don't have all day!"
"Shut it, they'll be quiet as the grave soon enough."

My heart beats fast and loud, my palms sweat. I can hear the men arguing, all the more frightening for the anger and evil in their quiet whispers. I know something horrific is happening and run to see what the problem is.

A small golden-haired puppy is picked up by a large gloved hand, no bigger than a child's football. He slips free only to be roughly captured again. He yelps in pain, then silence. Others are crying in fear, some bark in anger. I keep running, getting no closer. I feel the slippery stones beneath my feet. My chest tightens.

I'm cold with fear. Hot tears run down my face, one by one the puppies are silenced. NO! I cry out. They don't stop. The puppies are silent. I shiver uncontrollably; bury my head in my wet pillow.

"It's a dream...thank God it's only a dream." I sit up lightheaded and stagger to the bathroom. "Wow that was a bad one."

I often remember parts of my nightmare. Usually I'm being chased. This is new. I never wake up crying and sick to my stomach. I turn the faucet on and soak a washcloth in near scalding water and hold it to my face. The throbbing in my head eases but the fear in my heart remains. I can't stop shivering. All I remember is that I'm too late to save them but *who* are they and *where*.

I take a seat on one of the many stone benches placed at various spots around the park. I still feel the dregs of the nightmare. It's hanging on like a bad slasher movie, the kind that makes you feel weird for days. I hope the fresh air will help me feel better. I love to watch people. I always thought to sit and do nothing except watch people would be fun. It's not. It's *boring* after awhile.

There is something unique about Londoners. If we had this *soft mist* back home in Brooklyn, or what we call rain, folks would be rushing about wanting to get indoors. Here, these people act as if it's a sunny spring day. Take those three guys about to walk past my bench. They are strolling like they're not getting wet and here I'm holding an umbrella. I feel kind of silly, but this mist is wet. Hmm, that guy looks really dry. Wonder if it's that large, brimmed hat? Maybe I should get one. Even the hat looks dry, what gives with that? He's carrying a walking stick, and he looks as if he would like to use it on the other two. They're busy talking and don't seem to be paying him any attention, wonder if that's what's got his blood boiling?

The closer he gets the more he looks like that crime solving monk on BBC. His gray wool habit looks ancient and ragged, evidence of his vow of poverty. Around his waist is a rope with three knots tied in it. A large, old, wooden rosary and cross hang from it. He's also wearing leather sandals. Yuck, with these puddles, his feet must be soaked. I didn't think they wore habits like that anymore. I wonder if he has one of those monk-like hairstyles that look like fringe surrounding a bald spot.

The monk guy stops and stares at me. I feel a whispery chill and shiver. Did he catch me staring at him and get offended? I look away, stare at a tree and pretend to be absorbed in watching the light mist add a sparkle to the leaves. Yikes, he's coming over.

"Pardon me Miss. Can you see me?"

"Well yes, I'm really sorry; I didn't mean to stare. I'm a tourist." I stammer from embarrassment.

"You can really see and hear me?" He has a stunned look on his round, friendly face.

"Of course, shouldn't I?"

"No one has for a very, very long time. Let me introduce myself, I am Friar Francis Xavier from Hamptons Monastery."

"Oh, you're a Friar. I don't think I've ever met one before. What's the difference between a monk and a friar?"

"That is an excellent question. The short version of the answer would be that we go out among the people and the monks stay in. To whom do I have the pleasure of speaking?"

"Oh, I'm sorry, my name is Bridget. I'm from Brooklyn, New York, pleased to meet you," I extend my hand to shake his.

He just looks at my hand. "I am afraid I will be unable to shake your hand in greeting, although I have seen it done many times, I have never done it."

"Oh, I'm sorry, is it a rule of your order, no physical contact?"

"No, it is just that..." His light blue eyes look so sad. "I am.... well, how do I put this." He looks thoughtful, straightens his shoulders as if making a decision, "Here now, let me try..." He reaches for my hand, but his passes right through mine.

An icy wave of frigid air passes through my hand. I feel the burn as ice particles begin making their way through my body. I pull back quickly, but not fast enough. My hand begins to burn, and the cold makes me shiver. I look at my ghostly companion. His head is bowed, and I can feel an immense sadness pouring from him. I'm glad I held in my yelp of pain. Had this really happened or could it be my imagination run amok.

I look at the Friar. I can tell he didn't mean to hurt me. His solid form begins to fade, and parts of him are just shimmery light, I realize he's leaving. "That's okay we don't have to shake hands."

"You are not going to run from my presence?" With a bright light, he begins to take solid form again.

I begin chattering, "I'm surprised to meet a live ghost, well not *live*, but an English ghost, and I've only been in London less than a week. I guess it should scare me a little that you're a spirit, but it doesn't really. You see I'm Irish, and after meeting some folks in Ireland recently, nothing surprises me."

"Right then, may I visit with you a moment?"

"Of course, I'd love the company. I was just starting to feel lonely. Can you believe it? I'm so lucky to be in your beautiful city, why should I feel lonely."

What on earth am I doing talking about feelings to a stranger? Must be the monk's habit, I guess the fact that he's a ghost helps. Hey, who's he going to tell?

"Are you missing your family?"

"That's part of it. My best friend, Mary, well she's more like a sister, has found the love of her life and is busy meeting his family and touring England."

"Were you not invited to join them?"

"Oh, I was, but I'd feel like a third wheel."

"A *'third wheel'*? Yes, I see, as if you are intruding. Yes, very uncomfortable."

"That's it, uncomfortable is a good word. Simon is just wonderful, and I'm happy for her, but without Mary or even Mick, I feel lost."

"Is Mick your special fellow?"

I have to laugh at that. "Mick is special all right. Since you're a spirit, then you'll understand. Mick is a gift from my ancestors. He's a special talking dog that looks like an ordinary Brittney spaniel. He was sent to be my teacher or mentor into the world of the Fae folk."

"Did you say a talking dog?"

"Well he doesn't speak out loud, only in my head, sort of head to head conversation. He won't talk to just anyone, but I guess he would speak with you."

"Right then, I would be particularly interested in meeting your friend Mick. Where is he now?"

"He's still in Ireland. He said he would come over here someday soon. He does call me every day, well not on the phone, just in my head. He likes to check in to see how I am and what I'm doing. He is kind of an older brother, but with four legs."

Friar Xavier laughs along with me. He's easy to speak with, I soon find myself telling him of our time in Dublin. About meeting the Queen of the Fae and the King of the Leprechauns, and finding out that I'm related to them. How they asked for my help in saving the land. How I found a murderer, and uncovered a terrorist ring.

"Whoever knew that a dog would be such good company? Well there is that matter that he's a talking dog, which sort of helps I guess. Hmm, I wonder how many dogs talk to their owners, well maybe not as much as Mick, at least I hope not. That dog can really talk. I complained a lot about the constant chatter in my head as he went on and on with my 'lessons' but here I am, with hundreds of people around and I feel sad that I have no one to share this with. Well not anymore since you came along. I'm very happy to meet you Friar. Oh, sorry, should I address you as 'Father', as I would a priest?"

"Friar will be fine my dear. I believe your ancestors are correct in believing that you have many gifts. You have accomplished a great deal for one so young."

"I'm not that young. I'm almost twenty. Sorry I'm talking your ear off. I guess I'm a little lonely. I should feel excited. I'm sitting in a park, only a few hundred feet from Buckingham Palace, one of the most beautiful places in the world. It would be fun to talk to Mick about the palace. I can hear him now with that snooty tone of voice, 'Bridget, Buckingham Palace has been the official residence of the British Royal family since 1837.' Ah, he can be annoying but I really miss him."

"So here you are alone in a strange country."

"I came here with my friend Mary. We felt at home in London right away. New York has a lot in common with London, like the number of people, diversity of cultures, even the subway, or underground as you call it here."

"You like our city then?"

"Yes, we love it! We went to a few pubs, checked out Harrods and even went to their beauty shop. I had my brown hair streaked with blonde, and Mary had her hair cut so she could say she had it done at Harrods. We wandered about while Simon was finishing up work so he could take time off.

"Please don't get me wrong, I'm happy that Mary enjoys her English co-workers, and glad that Simon got some time away from the spy business to spend some time with her. But between her work and Simon, I just don't get to spend much time with her anymore.

"Mary would tell me that I need to enjoy the sights, but I don't seem to have the energy for it yet. Maybe tomorrow, I'm just so tired lately. What do people, who don't have to work for a living, do with their time?"

"Pardon me miss, may I be of assistance?"

I look up to see a guy in a midnight blue uniform. He's wearing a helmet with an emblem on it that has a crown sitting on a medal with the letters, 'EB'. A cop or what the English call a constable is looking at me with a puzzled look on his face. I realize that I'm talking out loud and no one will be able to see Friar Xavier.

"Sorry, I was just thinking out loud, everything's okay."

"Yes, miss, good day then." He touched his hand to his helmet and gave me that *cop* look. I wonder if all cops go to school to learn that *look*. It makes you feel guilty even if you aren't. Now that I think about it, the nuns who taught Mary and me had that *look* down pat.

I wait for the constable to walk off and turn back to Friar Xavier. "I'm sorry if I'm talking too much."

"Not at all my dear, please continue."

"I have a cousin here. He's the reason I came to London. I have to find someone to take over the land that I inherited in Ireland. I would prefer to find someone in the Carins family, who would love the land and take good care of it. You see, there is a faeire mound on the land that must not be disturbed.

"I finally found my cousin, with Simon's help, but he's out of town and not due back for a couple of days. So I'm just playing tourist. I'm glad you're here, it's nice to speak with someone."

I spot a couple who have stopped a few feet away and are looking at me. I guess all they can see is a girl sitting on a bench, in the rain, talking out loud. Before they call the constable or a shrink, I turn back to Friar Xavier and ask with my new head-talk skill, "Friar is it okay if we speak with our thoughts only?" I nod in the direction of the couple. "It might be less conspicuous and I love using my *Fae* talent."

♣♣♣

At that moment the young Fae are gathering at Stonehenge.

Interlude

Stonehenge

As the air stilled, the firelight drew giant shadows beneath the stones, which stand guard north of the small town of Amesbury, in Salisbury Plain.

Sound of neither voice nor wing could be heard as the eldest, untouched among us, opened the gold lined wood case that held the prophecy.

Over a hundred strong, we held our breath; dare we hope we will be saved? The Queen promised a way to rescue us. It is too late for our parents. Will help come before it is too late for us?

Emanon read the words to bring comfort and hope.

"When the darkness swells to encompass all that lies before it, one who is not of our land but of royal blood will come to learn, to battle, to stop the evil from spreading throughout the world.' "

"This is good news, Kasondra, don't cry."

"Que-tip, do you think there's hope?"

"We must all have hope, for without it, we are lost."

Chapter 2

Michelle

"Am I to understand that you may have some time on your hands at the moment? Would it be too presumptuous of me to ask for your assistance?"

"Of course not Friar, I would love to help you with anything."

"Now, this is a blessing. I was praying that someone could help me. My role is to keep the royal family content. I am their unseen counselor and can often aide them without their knowing. But this latest problem has me very worried for our dear Queen's health."

"What problem?"

"Have you read of the dog napping at her home in Sandringham?"

"Yes, it's in all the papers. It's so sad, I don't understand how folks can be so cruel. I heard they want some jewels. The Queen is worth millions. Can't she just give them the jewels and get her dogs back?"

"That is not her way. She will not bow down to the threats of criminals. Be that as it may, the jewels they want are not hers to give. They belong to the people. The ransom note specified the Crown Jewels."

"I'm planning on seeing them. They're on display at the Tower of London, aren't they?"

"Yes, you see, that is also part of this puzzle. On one hand, to take the dogs without being caught was clever. Yet to ask a ransom of something that the Queen cannot give, now that would make the persons who absconded with the Queen's dogs not very clever, or very, very clever indeed, do you see my problem?"

"Yes, I do," I answer, amazed by his mixture of old language, and modern day terms.

"Is that what you were doing just now, listening to those two gentlemen to see if you could find more clues?"

"Correct, and it is as bad as I thought. They are all pointing fingers at the French for causing this disaster. But that makes no sense. Why would one country want to cause unrest with another country, over something so insignificant to the world at large?"

"Well, it has been done many times in the past over things just as insignificant."

"Sadly, you are correct," he said as he shook his head from side to side, not wanting to accept the stupidity of man.

"Perhaps I can help, I'm not doing anything right now. What have you learned of the case so far?"

"I know that everyone is working on it and this little matter has the world's attention. The result is always the same. They seem to believe that the young French girl who was the veterinary assistant was the inside contact."

"They have to have some evidence to come up with that opinion. Do you know what it is?"

"The information I have is that Michelle was hired recently. She is the daughter of an English father and French mother who divorced when she was young. She was raised in France but would come over often to visit her father and assist him in his veterinary practice. She is attending the Royal Veterinary College part time, working on her degree in veterinary medicine. The men I was listening to are with MI5, they were saying that she is under surveillance and is now sitting on the steps of The Wedding Cake."

"The wedding cake?"

"Quite so," he smiles. "Queen Mum's Memorial is nicknamed "The Wedding Cake" as it represents the decoration on the top of one. In fact, if you get into a black cab, and ask to be taken to 'The Wedding Cake' many drivers will automatically take you here to the Victoria Memorial. It is just up ahead. Have you been that direction yet?"

"No, actually, I was about to go see Buckingham Palace, and now I have someone to share it with."

"It is a fine day for a bit of a walk. If you would like my, how shall I say, limited company. I would enjoy accompanying you and let you know a little of the story of The Wedding Cake. I so enjoyed watching it being built."

"Lead on Macduff," I said as I stood.

"Actually my name is..... Oh yes, Willie does have a few catchy phrases now doesn't he."

Wow, he calls Shakespeare, 'Willie', what better company than one who has witnessed so much history. Here I was beginning to get bored, and now I have another adventure. What is it that Mick would say, 'Life is an adventure, *Carpe Diem*. Seize the day!'

Friar Xavier walks beside me and begins to tell me some bits and pieces about the history of the area.

"In recent years much of the area around the Memorial has been made ready for pedestrians. From the steps of the Victoria Memorial you get great views. It was built in the time when Rule Britannia was a reality, and follows a nautical theme."

"I can't wait to see it."

"I will soon show you."

It sounds that, unlike Mick, this guy really enjoys playing teacher. Or it could be that he's also lonely, and likes talking to someone.

"Friar, how is it that you can travel about? From all I have read, spirits stay where their body is buried."

"Actually one, such as me, feels comfortable visiting those places that one visited most often. We are not limited at all. We may show up anywhere we choose. I am lucky in that, as a Friar who was in Royal favor, I visited many of the palaces in the area. William the Conqueror bequeathed the site that Buckingham Palace is built on to the monks of Westminster Abbey. Sandringham, and Hampton Court were also sites of monasteries at one time. You must visit Hampton Court Palace. It is the home of a very good friend of mine, Skeletor. He is quite famous. You might have heard of him?"

"No, I don't believe so. Why is he famous?"

"My friend is the famed CCTV ghost. 'Skeletor' is the name that was given to him after he appeared on a CCTV camera at Hampton Court Palace in October, 2003," he chuckles.

"Can you do that, just appear at will?"

With his blue eyes sparkling and a huge smile he explained. "Once in a great while, but the emotions have to warrant it. His emotions were very strong that day. It seems that a great many strangers were mucking about. He kept opening the door and they kept closing it. He lost his temper and appeared to scare them off. Since that fateful day many more visitors have come to Hampton Court Palace in hopes of catching a glimpse of the ghost."

"Poor Skeletor," I chuckled.

We're getting closer to the Palace and I can see parts of it through the trees. Friar Xavier continues his lecture and I find that I really enjoy listening to him. When we leave the shelter of the trees, I can see a crowd of people.

"Go on up the steps of The Wedding Cake for the best view," my new found friend and guide advises. "I need to pop in to check on the Queen."

I can hardly believe I'm standing on the steps of Queen Mum's Memorial in front of Buckingham Palace watching a ghost fly over the people and into the palace. This is unbelievable.

There are at least a hundred people around, all with cameras but standing on these steps I can still get a great view. I stand there in silence and give a prayer of thanks that I have this opportunity. Wait 'til I tell Mary, she has to see this. I can't wait to introduce her to Friar Xavier. She has met a talking dog but this will be her first ghost.

My companion of the last twenty minutes returns. I see him float down into the crowd. I look around and see him sitting on a step, next to an extremely thin girl. Her short cut burgundy tinted hair is streaked with black. I can't see her face; it's buried in her hands. Her shoulders are shaking as if she is crying. No one but Friar Xavier is sitting close to her. I guess people thought if they got too close her tears would intrude on their joy.

I go over and sit down next to her. The stone step is damp and cold. I reach into my satchel and turn to her, "would you like a Kleenex?"

Startled, she looks up and I can see what might be a beautiful face if it wasn't tear-stained and blotchy. Her eyes are red-rimmed and her nose is bright red. She looks as if she's been crying a long time. I hand her the small tissue pack I always carry. I take this opportunity to check her out as Mick has taught me to do. He explained that we all give off an energy signal. As one learns to read it, the signal will tell more about a person than they realize. Her aura is now mostly dark green and charcoal grey, which, according to Mick, shows she's depressed with mental stress. Mostly her aura is the aqua color of a healer and salmon pink, showing me a person who has found her true vocation. That reading and my gut tells me all that I need to know. She's innocent. She did not take the dogs. I hope MI5 has more suspects.

"*Merci,*" she takes one tissue and returns the package.

"Is there anything that I can do to help?"

"No, thank you. The Dorgis are missing," she cries.

"Doggies?"

"No no, my petite four Dorgis, my little Cider, Berry, Candy and Vulcan, but you know nothing; you are American!"

"Yes, I'm American. We do read the newspapers. Are you referring to the Queen's dogs that were taken from her home, what's it called? Oh yes, Sandringham House."

"*Oui*, ah yes, pardon. I do not mean to offend. Most tourists are too busy having fun to watch the news broadcasts or read the paper. I am, or should I say, *was*, the Queen's assistant veterinary at Sandringham House in charge of the Dorgis."

"Sounds like a great job."

"It was. The Queen was given a Corgi named Susan from whom numerous successive dogs were bred. Some Corgis were mated with dachshunds. Most notably the Corgi named Pipkin, who belonged to Princess Margaret, to create 'Dorgis'.

"The Dorgis are her pride and joy, they are *ce magnifique*." She buries her head in her hands again and continues to cry.

"Could you tell me what happened. I really do want to help if I can."

She lifts her head and looks at me, sniffles, blows her nose and says, "The Queen has entertained many a noted breeder at her home. It was during one of these 'showings' or how you would say, 'garden parties for dogs', that someone took the Dorgis. They think *I am* that someone."

"But why does everyone think you are to blame?"

"I was called to the phone and left them alone. They were safe in their cages in the old lodge. When I picked up the phone, no one was on it. I looked around for man who gave me message but he was not to be found. I search everywhere for him. He said my mother was on the phone and I wanted to know if she left him a message. You see, she is traveling in Africa and I cannot call her back. She is the only one whom I can speak to about all this and I cannot reach her."

Before she starts crying again, I ask more questions. "Were there other dog handlers in the old lodge when you left to answer the phone?"

"No, they were busy at the new kennel, it just opened this week. Everything is state of the art, all, what you say, high-tech. The same man who gave me the message to answer the phone at the main house was the man who told me that the Queen wanted my petites for a private showing. He was wearing a badge as a judge and I did not question him."

"So you didn't question a private showing at the old kennel?"

"No, the Queen has done that many times in the past. The old kennel is still set up for showings. It is not scheduled to be torn down until later this week. What does this all matter, they are gone," she cries.

I hand her another tissue. "My name is Bridget and I'd like to help you, if there is anything I can do. What is your name?"

"Ah *Oui*, my name is Michelle Beaulieu, what was your name?"

"I'm Bridget."

"Bridgette is a beautiful French name."

"It's Gaelic, my family came from Ireland. I come from the States."

"Oui, I can tell your accent."

"I'm sorry you are having problems, perhaps I can help?"

"No, it is I that is sorry for all the tears. I am asked to leave my post. This insufferable inspector, he tells me I am suspicious."

"You mean a suspect? They think you stole the puppies?"

"I didn't know where to go. I guess I am sitting here, wanting to see the Queen and let her know that I am innocent. She is a good lady. I know. Only good lady loves her Dorgis so much. They will not let me in." She nods in the direction of the Queen's guards.

"I have been trying all morning to see her. I know she is in there, see the pendant, it is flying. That means that she is here, but she will not see me. To her I am suspicious also." She places her face in her hands and cries again.

Yikes! I thought I was a watering pot when I was in Ireland but I couldn't have been this bad. I take another tissue from the pack and hand it to her.

"Here, the best thing to do is to dry your face and let's go someplace dry and have something to eat." Even with my rain coat on I can feel the damp of the cold, wet, stone step.

"I'm starving, how about you?" I stand up and wait for her to join me.

"Hey, whenever I have a problem, I know that any action is better than sitting still and worrying. Come on, let's go."

She stands to join me and I head for the line of taxis I see next to the street entrance.

"How would you like a pub lunch?"

She looks a little dazed but shakes her head in the affirmative. I wave at a black cab and ask him to take us to a local pub for lunch. Michelle may have thought it a little strange that I held the cab door open a little longer than usual as I wait for Friar Xavier to have a seat next to her before I join them. I think this ride will be a fun experience for the friendly Friar.

We're in luck. The cab drops us off within ten minutes, so the ride didn't cost too much. We're in front of a large two story pub. If I had to guess, I would say it was well over a hundred years old. No flashy signs, just a discreet old wooden sign above the door reads 'Thrasher Pub' in weathered, bright colored paint. If it wasn't for the sign, I would think that this was someone's home. Simon told me to always trust a cabbie to know the best places to eat. I open the large wooden door, darkened with age, to a color scheme of deep burgundies, browns, mustards and dark blues that blend together to give that great old English pub look I read about in the tourist guides. There are various seating options including leather sofas, or chairs. Along one long mirrored wall is a wooden bar with a brass rail and bar stools. The host greets us with menus in hand, dressed in a colorful vest and tie that work well with the surroundings. I think he asks us to follow him, but sometimes when the accent is strong, I'm never quite sure. He first shows us to a couple of leather chairs in front of the fireplace but I ask for a booth I spot in the back. A little more private in case Michelle loses it again.

I look over at her and she's checking out the old English decor. I look at Friar Xavier and burst out laughing. The good Friar is in mid-air staring at the large glass canisters of pickled eggs and what I hope isn't pig's feet. I don't think spirits eat or I would order some for him. Michelle looks to see what I'm laughing at and only sees the old time memorabilia on the walls.

"Let's get a seat."

A waitress in a dress that looks like it's straight from the fifties comes over to take our order. The menu is good and includes the history of the pub and a write-up on how they use farm fresh products including locally raised beef. We both order cheeseburgers. I order a Diet Coke and *Miss ninety pounds soaking wet* orders a milk shake. I'll never understand some people, they can eat anything and not gain weight. While we wait for the food we both look around at all the great paintings of medieval England and some village scenes with musicians. I'm grateful there are no paintings of dogs.

When the food arrives, I realize I'm starving. It must be all of the walking I've been doing. I'm halfway through my burger when I notice that Michelle is using a knife and fork to cut her burger into *itsy bitsy* little pieces before she eats it. *Wow, that's strange, but it may be why she's so thin and I'm still a size twelve.*

Michelle has a fashion model look. Her mahogany hair has a very expensive cut that emphasizes the pixie like features of her face. Even with the dark circles under eyes that are red rimmed from crying, she is beautiful.

She removes her very fashionable raincoat. Under it she is wearing a beautifully tailored piece, a bold black and red plaid with large bright red buttons, a black purse, and black patent leather boots with red bows. She dressed to meet with the Queen but I suspect she would look well dressed in whatever she wore. I love clothes and this outfit is fantastic. It must be a French number; I have never seen anything like it. It puts my herringbone jacket and black woolen slack outfit to shame.

I should really hate her. She even makes eating look like an art. I can't wait to tell Mary about her. Whoever heard of someone eating a cheeseburger with a fork and knife? She cuts a small piece of cheeseburger, puts down her fork and knife, then picks up her fork, places a tiny piece in her mouth. Puts down the fork, chews for so long you would think she has half of the burger in her mouth instead of a piece that would get lost on a teaspoon. Then she waits a minute or so before she starts the process over again.

She looks like she loves every bite and doesn't say a word the whole time she is eating. I look down at my half finished burger and the remaining ten percent of my fries and realize that she may be onto something. It looks like she is enjoying her food and I eat so fast, I don't remember really taking time to taste. Here this size two was taking time to enjoy every tiny bite. I start to pick up a fork but feel foolish. I grab my Coke and continue to watch her.

When she finishes about a quarter of her burger and just a few of the fries, she pushes her plate away and says, "That was very good, thank you for bringing me here. I was very hungry."

"You're welcome, I'm happy you like it."

"Are you on holiday here in London?"

"Yes, sort of a working vacation, I inherited farm land in Ireland that I would love to see go to a relative. I was told that I have a cousin here in London, but he's out of town at the moment, so I get to play. Hopefully he would like to move to Ireland and take care of the farm. I know nothing of farming and I need to get home, I guess."

"It does not sound as if you are very anxious to get home, but if you need help in seeing the sights, I could help you do that."

"Could you? That would be great. I've asked a few folks where to go but I couldn't understand a word they said. I think they were speaking English but the accent was different."

"You must have spoken to persons with a Cockney accent. It does cause one to listen very hard. It is sort of a rhyming slang."

I look next to her where Friar Xavier is sitting and see him shake his head.

"Actually instead of sightseeing, I would like to help you out if I can. Maybe we could go to Sandringham House and look around; you never know what we may find."

"You meant it; you really want to help me?"

"Sure, why not. I can tell that you didn't steal those dogs. You don't look much like *'Cruella De Vil.'*"

She has a puzzled look, "I guess you've never seen *'101 Dalmatians'* huh, don't know what you're missing. I love all the Disney shows."

"Ah Oui, she was the evil doggie nipper," she laughs briefly, "As if I could ever be an evil doggie nipper, I love

my little Dorgis," and begins to cry again. "It is no good; there is no help for me."

"Don't give up, let's just go there and try."

"You don't understand. I am not allowed anywhere near Sandringham or the Dorgis ever again."

"Oh, I forgot about that. We will think of someplace nearby to hide you."

I pay the check and the tip; surprised she didn't offer to help out. Oh well, I invited her and she's out of work at present. I have the money from the Irish lawyers, I can afford a lunch.

We put on our rain gear, open the large front door, and walk right into a downpour.

"Wow, now this *is* rain. No trip to the country today," I announce, and pull Michelle back into the café.

Michelle stands close and looks at me for a moment and asks "How old are you?"

When I don't answer her question right away she takes my chin in her hand, "What age?"

If she tries to pry my mouth open to check my teeth I'm going to belt her one. I pull away and say, "Nineteen, I'll be twenty in October. Why, what's up?"

"Old skin, you do not take good care of yourself. We go to spa and get pampered. What do you say? You need facial for old skin."

"*Old skin*, what the...."

But she's no longer there to argue with. Next thing I know I am being pulled back out into the downpour. I watch her hail a cab and give the address to the driver. I guess I am on the way to get treatment for my 'old skin'.

I look over at Friar Xavier and he is smiling. *"I will return to the Palace and check back with you in a couple of days."*

Great, no help from him, I guess his travel adventure doesn't include a beauty spa.

Chapter 3

Taken by a French Spa

"Bridgette finish drying, they have made room for us."

Michelle has already reached the second floor and I hurry to catch up. I almost trip up the steps as I try to take in the crystal chandelier. Where on earth are we?

I realize that folks respond to stress in different ways. I guess Michelle's idea of dealing with a charge of dog-napping and the loss of her job is to spend money at a spa but I can't afford this place.

Before I know what's happening, Michelle is gone. I'm led to a dressing room and handed a robe made of the same extra thick white terry cloth as the towel. What on earth? They're giving me a facial right? Why do I need a dressing room and a robe?

"Are you ready?"

I open the door to tell Michelle to *forgetaboutit*. She stands there all in white; her hair is covered in a white turban, she is wearing white fuzzy scruffs with a matching robe. All that is noticeable is her big smile.

Okay, I guess I can do this, "I'll be right there." I close the door and hurry to get out of my clothes.

My lady, whose name tag reads, Audrey, puts a fluffy white washcloth on my face. I take a deep breath and begin to relax. Too soon, Audrey gestures for me to follow her to another room with two large white leather armchairs that are sitting on a pedestal. In front of the chairs are mini hot tubs.

Audrey tells me to have a seat just as Michelle comes into the room. "How did you like your facial, wasn't it heaven?"

"It was an adventure. Thank you, but what's with the chair."

"One must have a pedicure on a day like this."

"But I never…"

"Sit. Put your feet in the tub, you will love it."

I did as instructed and then realize why the chair is so big and well constructed. The dang water is so hot that I scream and push back. I guess I would have tumbled a smaller chair. I pull my poor feet out. They are beet red.

"You will adjust to the temperature. Come put your feet back in," says my spa Nazi. Maybe she did take the dogs, she has a mean streak.

Michelle is right and my poor red feet adjust to the heat. A lady in black comes in and hands us each a flute of clear sparkling liquid.

I thank her and ask Michelle, "What's this?"

"It is champagne of course, a good year." She says with approval, looking at the date on the bottle left on a little black table between us.

I am relaxing and thinking how much I have to tell Mary. She will get a great laugh at me, of all people, drinking champagne and getting treatments in a spa. I'm glad I came along with Michelle. I take a sip of this 'wonderful' champagne and try not to grimace. *Champagne is way overrated. It tastes like diet ginger ale.*

The facial looks like it helped Michelle feel better. Her face looks great and she seems much more relaxed. She giggles and reaches over to play with the buttons on my chair.

"What are you doing?"

"These chairs are *ce magnifique*! You will see."

Soon the chair begins to heat up and what feels like metal balls begin to move up and down my spine.

"Wow that does feel wonderful." Now if I wasn't so embarrassed by having a girl my age sitting at a low stool in front of the wash basin, picking up my foot and washing it.

OH MY GOSH, I forgot to shave!! Hoping no one will notice I ask the foot lady her name. *That's it lady, look at my face while we talk and don't notice my hairy legs.*

Of course she puts white cream all over my leg and all the tiny stubs of hair now look an inch long. The black hairs stand up like solders at attention. I just want to die. I keep trying to get my leg out of her hands and back under the water but she holds on like a pit bull.

The heck with it, I'm paying for this madness. Why should I allow anyone to embarrass me? I pour myself a full glass of champagne and begin to enjoy myself. That's until the water demon starts to use a block of sandpaper on the bottom on my foot. I jump so high, I not only spill the champagne again but the flute goes flying and crashes against a fancy glass case. I have ten pounds to lose but there is no way I could have knocked that chair over. What's going on?

Michelle is right behind me when I leave. She's crying again.

"I'm so sorry Michelle. I didn't mean to embarrass you. I paid for the damage."

"It is not you. When they ran my credit card and notice my name, they told me that I am an embarrassment to all France and I would never be welcome in their establishment again."

I put my arm through hers and we walk down the fresh rain-washed street.

"Hey girl friend, at those prices, you can hire yourself a fulltime maid."

She doesn't laugh so I pick up an empty Coke can off the street and back hand it into the corner trash bin. When it misses, I give it a puzzled look, "Darn, it worked with a champagne flute."

She looks at my serious face and bursts out laughing. "You Americans, you are crazy in the head."

"You may be right, but that's what makes us lovable."

We both laugh and talk over my first spa experience. We walk and plan our trip to the country for the following morning.

As we near the Underground, I feel something's not right. The hairs stand up on the back of my neck, as if I'm being watched. I look around but don't see anyone. I take a deep breath and realize why I feel so spooked; whatever is watching us is not friendly, and not human.

Interlude

Morrigan *

Mick materializes in the dining hall and approaches the King and Queen as they converse with members of the court.

"What is the meaning of this interruption, My Lord?"

"A thousand pardons My Lady, it could not be helped. I have just learned from my young charge that she has met Morrigan, and I fear for her life."

Padraig gave a slight nod, the court fades from view. The three are now in private chambers. Queen Geraldine stands and the walls shake with her fury.

"Tis not possible, we have kept her safe, and away from all magic, how could this have happened?"

"It was in the caves My Lady, while I was last in your presence. Bridget changed her routine. She decided to rise early, and play detective on her own. She found her way to the caves beneath the old fort. Morrigan was visiting the wee folk in the area."

"Are you telling me that our Bridget escaped my cousin unharmed?"

- * *Book One - The Brooklyn Leprechaun*

"Not completely My Lady, she was bruised. I still do not understand how she escaped death by Morrigan."

"This will not happen again. We must prepare her. Keep her out of any contact with our kind. Let her be a tourist in London as you continue to teach her more of her gifts. Observe what other talents come to the surface. It seems that there may be more to the child of our blood than even we are aware of."

"Hmm, that is another thing My Lady. Your descendent has the ability to move the Fae affected by your cousin, to Cathcaruth, where as you know, they will stay until such time as Morrigan's power has been removed from your kingdom."

"My Lord, we have heard of these incidents, but assumed you had moved your teachings far beyond the basic," said Padraig.

"You are saying that Bridget has the power to see, and banish my Fae naturally, this is not a power you have taught her?"

"That is correct my lady. Bridget is a remarkable young woman and I believe she may have a great deal of talent that we have yet to observe."

"Could it be possible? Could the full gifts of both her Leprechaun and faeire ancestry be surfacing in this human child after so many generations have passed?" Padraig questioned.

"That does seem to be the case," a delighted Geraldine responds. "Then my dear Lord Howth, you must go and prepare her for the battle that lies ahead. Keep her from all harm, she is our only hope."

A court attendant materializes next to Padraig, "Pardon me your majesties, my Lord. An urgent missive has arrived that requires your attention." He hands a scroll to the King and vanishes.

"Lord Howth you may have help in the care of our dear Bridget. It seems she now has the full support of the Fae children that have yet to be placed under the Morrigan spell. They have gathered under the stones, and read the prophecy. They believe as we do, that she is the one foreseen to rescue us all."

"How on earth did she...?" Lord Howth shifts into his guise of Mick pauses and turns his head to the side.

Chapter 4

Home to Battersea

I wave goodbye to Michelle and laugh as she yells *"Cheerio."* With her strong French accent it sounds more like *Sherry-o*.

Michelle hails a cab for her trip home. I walk down the well lit stairs to enter the tube station for my 30 minute trip to Battersea. My timing's terrible, the station's packed. Luckily I don't have to wait long because the trains run every five minutes.

I can't shake the feeling I'm being watched. No one seems to be paying me any attention. I've put up with crowded platforms and eccentric folks for most of my life. Doesn't mean I like it.

My stay in Ireland opened my eyes to another world. I can't believe I fell in love with country living in such a short time, maybe it is my Fae family. Heck, I miss them all. And I'd much rather drive than take a train, but parking in the city is a major hassle.

Okay, let go of the fear. Mick is not the only one that taught me to always be aware of my surroundings. Growing up in the hood is a major lesson in survival. Fear will only get in the way. I reach out to see if I can pinpoint the source of my unease. There it is, by the bench, not a shadow but the absence of one. Like a blank space where there shouldn't be one. I walk over and say, *"Be gone with ye now and don't come back."*

It's gone. Thank goodness Nana's old saying works here. In Ireland I didn't feel the fear, I wonder what has changed.

"Your awareness of the seen and unseen will one day rescue you from a depth of pain you could never have imagined. Trust with your heart."

The odd whispery words from an unknown female tread over me, sending a shiver down my spine. I take some deep breaths to calm down. It isn't that I don't feel safe alone in train stations. Mary's mom always made sure we knew how to protect ourselves. The self defense training she dragged us to will stay with me forever.

I reach into my purse for my train pass and move my wallet to my pants pocket. My keys with the mace canister attached goes into my coat pocket for easy access. The train is packed solid, the volume of voices high with a variety of accents.

The seats are all taken and I have to stand. I don't think it will be for too long. I know many people get off at Trafalgar Square. As we approach the station, people begin to gather their belongings to switch to other train lines or to get a bus.

I spot a seat by the window. Two rows of double seats that face each other are more comfortable than the long bench of seats with people on both sides standing over you. I race over to the recently vacated seat, sit and look out the window. It's so familiar. I begin to relax as I look out at the darkness of the tunnels as we race by. I can just let my mind drift.

Hard to imagine we're under a major city. The tunnels are a city beneath the city, a world of their own. In a strange way the movement has a mesmerizing effect and I soon begin to really relax and yawn.

I don't know why I'm so tired. Maybe it's because the day started early with a friendly ghost and then a French nut case whom I feel connected to. I wonder why. Michelle is rude, a little arrogant and an 'in your face' personality. Hey, she could be a New Yorker.

Maybe it's the same with all folks from large cities. We have our own unique identity and don't see anything wrong with it. She does *push it* a little, like that *'old skin'* comment, what's with that? I'm glad we stopped for tea somewhere quiet, she's really shook up. I don't think she would hurt a flea. Don't know why they blame her. Wonder what evidence they have.

How on earth am I going to help her? Well no matter, it's more fun than waiting for my cousin Peter to get back from Holiday. Glad we had that nice long talk about Sandringham, how things work, what her job was. A lot of things are beginning to make more sense.

I pull out my notebook to record all that happened to me today. Hard to believe it was just a few hours ago that I met Friar Xavier and wound up promising that I will go to Sandringham tomorrow and see what could have happened to the Dorgis.

I don't think Michelle will be much help, she's way too upset. The major problem is, who took the Dorgis and why do they want to frame her. Okay, first my list:

What does this place look like?

What evidence do the police have?

It must be *something* good for them to tell her not to leave the country. Can't be *too* bad or they would've put her behind bars already.

She's so upset that the manager of the spa asked her not to return. Did her own countrywomen suspect her or they just don't like the bad press? Think it will hurt business? Whatever happened to innocent until proven guilty? Or is that just in America? Well even there we tend to believe all that we hear on TV, or read in the newspapers.

I close my eyes and listen to the sounds around me as the train continues racing towards Battersea. The crowds are beginning to thin out. The sound of the conductor saying *"Mind the Gap"* is the only difference between a New York City subway and the tube.

My mind continues to wander as I hear folks getting off to go home. That will be me again one of these days, up early, race to work, race home to run errands, get everything done, just to do it all again the next day. My inheritance won't last very long and I will be back in the grind. Will I have to return to Brooklyn without Mary? Guess I can afford to go to school full time now. Maybe work some temp job in the evenings. Well, can't think of that now. Like Mick would say *'Carpe Deme'* seize the day... enjoy each minute. I open my eyes and look again at my notebook. The page has flipped back to my list from yesterday.

#1, Meet with Peter to see if he would like to take over the land.

That's certainly still my priority but I can keep busy while I wait. I promise myself that the very first thing I must do is to find a relative to take over the land in Ireland. It *can't go out of the family.* Can't imagine it sold to a developer. What if they built a Mickey D's on it? I'd be haunted the rest of my life and beyond. Anyway, if they tried to move the faeire mound all sorts of bad luck might befall them. Hmm, I wonder how my new family would like haunting an old apartment building in Brooklyn. Hey, some of the tenants wouldn't notice anything different about them.

Guess there's a lot I don't know about spirits. My great, many, many times great grandmother might be Geraldine the Queen of the Faeire, but she's not very highfalutin for a queen. I had to smile when she said "call me Grace," and my old granddad "Padraig." For the King of the Leprechauns, he is a funny character ... I wonder if they can leave the land in Ireland, wonder if they're trapped in Ireland because they're royalty.

What the heck do I know about *real* ghosts, only ones I know about are all actors on television or the old *Casper* the Friendly Ghost comics. Well, I guess I am going to learn more about real ghosts. At least they don't need passports. I chuckled.

The guy next to me turns and smiles, "Here you go luv, have a look see," he gets up to leave and hands me the paper he'd been reading.

Oops, he must think I was reading over his shoulder and read something funny, "Ah, thank you that will be great."

I hold the paper for a second and watch as he leaves the train. Nice guy, more Mary's runner boy type then mine. I open the London Times to the front page and read the headlines in shock. "French Connection Proven" *GOOD GRIEF, a warrant has been issued for Michelle.*

Dang, they say that they can't locate her. Expect that she may have left the country. Noooo, we were in a spa, boy these news guys love to make up news. I guess exciting assumptions sell newspapers. What can I do? She'll walk right into the hands of the police when she gets home. Well I figured I had to solve this by myself, but now she won't even be available for a cup of tea and a chat.

I look up as a slender, tall lady, possibly in her forties, moves from her seat across the aisle to sit in the seat facing me. She looks very attractive in a vintage black overcoat with grey fur on the collar and cuffs. Wow, that coat must have cost a mint. I think that's real chinchilla. Her blonde hair is done up in a French twist and a much sought after, vintage box hat with a peek-a- boo veil, sits at a cocky angle to give her a jaunty appearance. She leans towards me. "Couldn't help seeing the headlines, what do they think of the French in the states?"

As she waits for my answer, she sits back in the seat, takes out her knitting, finds the spot where she stopped, and looks back up at me expectantly.

"I really don't hear very much about them. We love all things French. They're still the final word in fashion. The French men you see on television are always so sexy, what's not to like?"

"I am very familiar with the French people. The Americans and English do not understand them. The French say that Americans smile all of the time, for them, there must be a reason to smile. *'Someone who smiles all the time is not to be trusted.'* For them it is hard to understand.

"Our countries do not constantly worry about invasion. For more than two thousand years the French have been invaded by one country or another. So they are wary of strangers.

"I may have been born in Florence, Italy, but I am a true Englishwoman who has seen her share of war. Yes, one should be very wary."

"I guess most folks do not really understand the French people. Heck, most folks don't understand us New Yorkers."

"New Yorkers have very strong personalities, they are very outgoing. French people are not overly outgoing. They like to take their time to get to know you. They do not understand a stranger shouting, "Hey mister, where is the Eifel Tower?" To them it is rude. Even in an emergency one is taught to be polite. One says *'Excusez-moi de vous d'eranger madam,'* which simply means 'excuse me for disturbing you madam'. Then ask your question."

"That's not our way. Maybe that's why folks who don't understand us, call New Yorkers rude."

She looks up from her knitting and stares at me for a second. The look in her silver blue eyes is so piercing. It feels as if they are performing a Vulcan mind meld.

She nods her head as if accepting what I said. "The French have 2,000 years of history that have made them mistrustful of strangers. It should be *mandatory* for all government officials to learn history. We should all learn from our mistakes."

I look up as the train slows and realize that this is my stop. "I wish I didn't have to get off, it was a pleasure speaking with you. Bye."

I race to the door before it closes. I hear her say, "You are welcome Bridget, always question until you find the answer that feels right for you. Good luck with your search."

I step off the train to the loud announcement to *"Mind the Gap."* As I turn and look back, to wave at my traveling companion, she is *gone*.

Hey, she called me by name. Who was that, was she another spirit? I would have loved to talk to her for hours. Why are spirits appearing to me? Not as translucent images but like real life, skin and bones people. *What's with that?*

I stare at the retreating train, and all of a sudden I feel my skin crawl. Something evil is close. I'm terrified. Two hands push against my back, and I'm flying towards the train tracks. From the corner of my eye I see another train approaching. *I'm going to die* and the only thing I can think about is that I never got to see the inside of Buckingham Palace.

Suddenly I feel a sharp tug on my raincoat, and two strong hands pull me back to the platform. I sit on the ground shaking.

"Aw you right then Miss? Want me to call someone for you?"

I look up into the eyes of a short brawny guy dressed like a construction worker. All I can do is shake my head.

"Don't be standing so close to the edge Miss, these here platforms can be dangerous. Here you go then."

He helps me to my feet and I finally get out two words, "Thank you."

Chapter 5

The Flat

I turn the corner onto East Street. I love this neighborhood. This is a vibrant neighborhood. It's peopled by people with history, by up-and-coming immigrants, students and artists. It might not be real ritzy, but it's full of hope. These people are looking forward, toward the future. So different from some of the neighborhoods I've lived where people live in fear and despair.

I see a black cab pull up in front of the door to the flat I'm using. I move a little faster hoping its Mary, but then a man comes out closes the back door and leans in the window to hand the driver the fare. He's tall and built like a bodyguard, all muscle. He has on a dark blue shirt that's open at the collar, the cuffs rolled up on strong forearms. From this angle I couldn't help but notice his form fitting designer jeans. He looks hot.

Since it is no one I know, I continue walking to the front door of my street level flat.

"Pardon me, would you be Bridget?"

"Yes I am," I say as I turn to greet the newcomer. I immediately recognize him as a Carins. This great looking guy must be Peter. He looks a lot like my father, with his dark black curly hair and deep, dark brown eyes.

"Peter?"

"Yes, I am pleased to finally meet you," he says as he stands there with his hand raised. I think he's undecided whether to shake my hand or give me a hug.

I rush over and hug him and feel my eyes tear up. Here is a blood relative. I believed, for most of my life, that I was alone. I had friends but no family. Of course I met Geraldine and Padraig but it's hard to hug ghosts.

"I'm so happy you are here. Would you like to come in for a cup of tea?"

"I would love one. I am so sorry to come over so late. I will only stay a few minutes. I could not wait any longer to make your acquaintance."

I drop my purse and keys on the small table in the entrance hall and gesture to Peter to join me in the living room.

"I'm happy you came over. I really wanted to meet you."

He smiles, gets a little red in the face and busies himself looking around.

"This is a great flat. I have been looking for something like this. Does it come with a garden?"

"Yes I really enjoy it. Simon's friend has a neighbor that's watering it while he is out of town. It's beautiful back there. I sit there often and enjoy my tea. It's a perfect location, just off the kitchen."

"Wish it was light out, I would love to see it. For tonight the front parlor will be grand. We have so much to talk about. I know I should have called first but as soon as I got home and received your message, I had to come over."

"Have a seat. I'll put on the kettle."

When I return with the tea, Peter is looking at the picture of Grandma Prendergast. The way he is staring at it, I think he might recognize the large painting she was standing in front of when the picture was taken.

"Nice picture isn't it?"

"Pardon? Oh the picture. Certainly, it is nice. Is this a relative of yours?"

"She is the lady who raised me for a few years after my mother died."

Peter sits on the straight back chair across from the sofa. There is a long silence, both of us not knowing what to say. It isn't everyday you get to speak with a cousin you never met. I finally break the silence, "How was your holiday?"

"My holiday was not your typical vacation. I was working."

I wait an uncomfortable couple of minutes and then ask, "What kind of work do you do?"

"That's sort of a long story. Have you inherited any gifts from our ancestors?"

I think I know where this was heading but I'm not sure if I'm ready for it. "What kind of gifts do you mean?"

"For example there is a strong gift of divination, of seeing the future. Some people call it intuition, I just know some things. There are actually millions of people with this gift, although most choose to ignore it."

I'm ready to tell Peter of my recent experiences, but he continues speaking.

"When I was a kid I never knew what a strong intuition was or what it meant. Then when I got older and could read the papers, I saw a headline with a picture that could have come directly from my dreams. I was lucky that I spoke with an uncle who knew of the 'gift', and let me know what it meant. I guess it comes to some of us in the family. A way of seeing the future, and we can decide to do something about it, or not. It is up to us."

I thought of my on-going nightmare of running away and knowing something is hunting me. I give myself a mental kick to focus on Peter, and ask, "What kind of things have you seen over the years?"

"Well it started out small. I would see a kid I knew crying over a lost dog, and then I would see the dog trapped in an old shed. As I got older, the demands of my gift have gotten harder. I became a private investigator to work as my cover to meet with people, and return their lost items, or rescue children from kidnappers, those kinds of things."

"That's fantastic. You must love your work. I guess now is a good time to tell you why I wanted to get in touch, besides just wanting to meet you."

I tell Peter my long story about Ireland. Winning the contest, getting to finally see the land I inherited, and my wish that it will be kept in the family. I'm hoping he will get excited and volunteer to move to Ireland right away, but he is quiet and keeps looking at me under those dark heavy eyebrows.

I ask, "So what do you think?"

"I am glad we found one another but I have a special job here that I must do. Ireland is not for me. Have you met any of the Irish relatives?"

Now what do I tell him? That I met our ancestors and they are Fae? He will lock me up and throw away the key.

"I met my uncle's wife on my mother's side of the family."

He looks at me again, and I feel as if he was making up his mind to tell me something extraordinary. "Have you ever been told faeire stories?"

"What kind of faeire stories?"

"This is not easy to talk to anyone about. It would be easier if I knew what were your feelings on…well what some people refer to as special magical gifts."

"So you know about our ancestors?"

"What do you know?"

I explain how I recently met my greats, and the Fae folk.

"Do you have other gifts?"

"Not that I know of, just my one gift since childhood. Being able to see into the future is a great gift sometimes. I knew you were coming to London. I also know that you will help me stop the bombing of St. Paul's Cathedral.

"Stop the what?" I jump up and pace around the room. "Is this another dream you know will happen? Do you know when this is going down? Will it happen soon?"

"The dream is coming back more often; it has always been like this. When I have a dream about something of importance and it comes to me often and then almost daily, it will happen soon, I know it.

"This time I saw you, coming from over the seas and helping me. It is strange to know that I have someone to help. I really don't know what to do. I have never had this big of a challenge to deal with."

"So tell me all the details, how you see this coming down."

"I am in what looks like an abandoned tube station and there are men loading packages of C4 onto an old handcar like you see in the movies, the kind that the old miners used. Then I see St. Paul's in a million pieces."

"We can't let that happen! How are you going to stop it, I haven't a clue what to do, but if I can help I will try my best. Do you have any ideas?"

"I believe what I am seeing is an abandoned tube station. I will need a map of all tube stations and will need to check out those that are no longer in use."

"Sounds simple enough but it will take a lot of time."

"Problem is I can't locate any abandoned stations. There is no such listing on-line, just active stations. I really feel as though we don't have much time."

"Even if we find a map we will need to narrow it down to tube stations around the cathedral. Why would someone close down a perfectly good tube station in the heart of the city?"

"I agree it doesn't make much sense."

"I'm sorry Peter; I need to head out of town for a little project I'm working on. As soon as it's done, I promise to help one hundred percent of my time."

"No problem Bridget. I will keep trying to locate the abandoned tube station."

"I will think about it also. What is your cell number? I'll call you if I think of anything."

Chapter 6

Sandringham

My thoughts wander as I lean over the salmon colored, stone sink to wash my hands. Good thing Michelle drew me a map of the grounds last night. I just knew I shouldn't have had that third cup of tea this morning. It takes forever to find a john around this place. She could have mentioned the *WC* on the map stood for 'water closet,' the English name for a bathroom.

Wow, Sandringham is popular! There has to be two dozen tour buses here. I park at least a mile away from the entrance. The Sandringham Estate is gi-normous. According to the literature it covers twenty thousand acres which includes six hundred acres of woods and the Country Park. The house itself is set in sixty acres of gardens. I stop and take pictures along the way. The Norfolk Coast region is so beautiful it takes your breath away. Wait till Mary sees some of the shots. She'll add this place to her must see list.

It's funny I feel as if I'm being watched. Wonder if they have a camera in the restrooms in case someone does something stupid, like mark this beautiful old stone, nah that would be just too weird.

I look at my reflection in the mirror. I think walking and fresh air is doing some good. I used very little make-up this morning.

Wonder if it's from feeling more alive when I'm on an adventure. Heck even my brown eyes are shining. Maybe it's from my sassy new hair style. I shake my head and watch

What *the heck is that?* In the mirror from this angle, I can see the top of the swinging door to the stall I just left. There is a little person, *a faeire*, sitting up there watching me. She is dressed in a sky blue and silver weave body suit. The belt has the same sapphire colored rhinestones that are on the band holding her hair. Wow, her hair looks like a squashed cotton ball.

"Hi, are you a London faeire?"

I continue looking in the mirror. I don't want to turn around, and scare her off. I swallow a laugh as I watch her slip from her perch in shock. She doesn't fly away. She places her right hand to her hair, like an old time cowboy patting his sidearm, straightens her shoulders and flies over to sit on the paper towel dispenser, so she could *almost* look me in the eye.

'Hi, my name is Bridget."

"I am called Que-tip, but don't get any ideas of zapping me away. I am not as easy a push-over as those two in Ireland."

"Oh, you heard about those. Well I can explain, or at least I think I can."

"Go on then."

"When my friend Mary and I unpacked our things at the flat in London, I found a picture of my Grandma Prendergast. She's the lady who raised me for a couple of years after my mom died. In the picture, she's standing in her living room. On the wall behind her, is a painting of the faeire, she would tell us stories about. It all came back to me then. The two in Ireland that I thought were figments of my imagination, were real and, I... ah wished them away. Did I hurt them?"

"Not bloody likely, we are immortal, they are in a holding place where they can do no more harm until Queen Geraldine releases them."

"That's great. I wouldn't want to hurt them. I have a million questions, and my mentor Mick hasn't shown up yet to answer them."

Just then I hear some women coming, "Is there some place private we could go and talk?"

"Sure, I'll ride along. Your hair is long enough to hide me. Loosen it from that horse tail."

"Sure," I laugh, pulling the rubber band from my hair. "We call it a pony tail, same idea."

As soon as I have my hair loose this cute little faeire flies to my shoulder, and makes herself comfortable. I cover her with my hair, turn and open the door. There are three ladies who are laughing and talking in a language I didn't recognize. I don't think they even see me hold the door open for them, no mind a three inch faeire on my shoulder.

We leave the old stone building that has been remodeled to house the public facilities.

"Which way?"

"You are here to see where the dogs were taken, everyone is. *Gawkers* we call them. Pay decent money to gawk at other peoples troubles. Well you won't get close you know, it is cordoned off."

I look over to where another bus load of tourists is heading down the gravel path. "Well that can wait for now. We can go to my car, no one will hear us talking there."

"They can't see me when I shield, at least no one, except those with a touch of Fae. I thought it would be fun to ride. You must have more than a touch of Fae is what I am thinking."

I didn't bother to answer that comment. I really don't know how to. I return to the parking lot and find my little rental car. I walk to the left hand side but notice my mistake before I unlock the door. I can hear a distinct laugh in my ear like the twittering of a bird.

"Okay smarty. This whole steering-wheel on the wrong side messes me up a bit."

After I unlock the driver's door and sit behind the steering wheel, I push my hair back to allow my guest to fly to the dashboard.

"Now, before we talk, let me make this clear. You zapped those Irish faeire by accident?"

Que-tip has her hands on her hips, chest puffed out and an expression on her face that says she did not believe anyone could be that stupid.

"Yes, it was fully by accident. Perhaps if my father hadn't moved away from the Prendergast family, I might have learned more. I had dinner with one of their sons once. The oldest, his name is Thomas, but I lost track of Peggy and the others. I heard that they moved to Texas. All I have now are more questions and unless I go back to Ireland and fall into a fairy mound again, I don't know how to reach Geraldine or Padraig. Mick said he would come *if I needed him.* I just need to call his name. He is my mentor sent by Geraldine. I really miss him but I don't want to bring him to a city when he can run free in the country, especially when I really don't *need* him."

The little faeire is looking very puzzled. I continue with my questions.

"If you can shed some light on this I really would appreciate it. Mick never mentioned faeire. He was working on making me aware of my gifts and inner strength so that I would stop being scared and worried all of the time. So, what do I need to know of faeire and how do I have the power to zap them?"

"Right you have it. First off my name is...." She pauses "they call me Que-tip," absently patting her large pure white afro that really did resemble the cotton top of a Que-tip.

I notice she still did not tell me her full name, still not completely trusting me. Maybe she's thinking if I knew her full name I could zap her. Heck I didn't use a name to zap the other two. I just told them to *be gone* and not come back.

"There is a story going about... and when isn't there, I'd like to know."

She sits Indian style and then just floats up so that I could see her better. I have a flashback to watching Tinkerbelle in Disney's Peter Pan and stifle another laugh.

Well I'm sure not lonely or bored now. Just watching the expressions on her very animated face is priceless. She has a pointy little face with high cheekbones, an awesome number of freckles on a shiny pale face, a generous mouth with teeth that had a little gap in the front two and a sharp little nose.

Her tightly curled white hair is held in place by a ring of colorful rhinestones. She has so much hair it hides her ears. I wonder if her ears are pointed at the top. She is a natural actress, puts her whole body behind each expression and is a kick to watch.

She continues, "According to the latest tale, it would seem that a long lost relative of our good Queen Geraldine has been found. She alone has the power to release us from Morrigan and return our Queen to full immortal life. Of course we all have heard this story before and have little hope but lately we have also heard stories of someone who can send M.F.'s to the holding place. Now that has us really interested. It is the first time we have heard that story."

"What are M.F.'s?"

"Why, M.F. stands for Morrigan Followers, of course. Not that they have any choice. The spell hits all fairy folk above the age of reason, or as *you* would say the mortal age of twenty one. When we turn twenty one we are compelled to spread the disease of hatred and ill will. Can't you tell it is getting stronger every year?"

"But how do they do this?"

"Simple really, my parents are a grand example. My father is assigned to the Page of the Chambers. The Page of the Chambers is responsible for the preparation of the State rooms, for stage-managing the ceremonial aspects of all functions, including The Queen's daily audiences, receptions, investitures and appointments. He is also in charge of serving arrangements at receptions and on other occasions. All that my poor father has to do is start a rumor. Something negative that makes the Page out of sorts for the day. Then the entire staff that is involved tending to the royal guests and overseeing the preparation of guests' apartments will be out of sorts. In one way it is fun to watch. One person's disposition can have a major impact on the lives of others."

She must notice the puzzled look on my face because she continues to explain.

"One day my dad starts a downright nasty thought going around in the bosses' head. He snaps at his second in command, who snaps at his assistant, and eventually the entire section is out of sorts, and the Queen has a problem that no one can explain. Strong negative vibes are harmful. They affect morale and can affect health in humans. There are hundreds working the palace. Each visits with a head of state if they don't already have one assigned. We are worldwide you know. Morrigan loves all the subtle and direct ways we are used to spread her message."

"Something tells me that she started out in the Middle East."

"What's that you say?"

"Nothing, please go on with your story."

"My brothers have a harder job; they are assigned the couriers to the Princes. Now they are a handful. Can you imagine getting them to be negative?"

"Okay back-up. What was that you said about Morrigan? I met a Morrigan in the caves in Mayo. Who is she and how on earth am I going to stop her when she has the whole Fae kingdom in her control?"

"You met Morrigan, and are alive to tell about it! Wait till I tell the NLFFT's about that."

"The *what?*"

"My homies. The Nice Little Fae Folk Tribe."

"*Homies,* where on earth did you hear that term? That's U.S. slang."

"At the county park," she points with her body to the woods, at the right of the parking lot.

"It has a place for caravans. We gather at night and listen to the young ones. When you meet with us, you will hear a variety of languages."

"When I meet you?"

"Sure, how else are you going to take care of Morrigan without your own army of faeire? We can help; just tell us what we need to do."

"Tell *you,* what *you* need to do! Who on earth will tell *me?*"

I put my hand up to stop her saying anything more until I can take it all in. So that's what's behind all of this training. Why didn't Mick or my greats tell me? They don't genuinely want to help me just because I'm family, they want something from me. They want to use me somehow. I don't think I want to learn what it is right now. With my luck, they probably want to feed the yank to the evil Morrigan.

"Que-tip, I have a headache right now *(actually the pain is lower than my head).* I'm going to drive to Kings Lynn, I saw an advertisement for hotels, and I want to find a hotel room for the night. That four hour drive tired me out. What time do the crowds die down around here?"

"Seven P.M. is a fair bet. You want me to meet you then for a private tour?"

"Let's make it much later, how about, Four A.M? I want to make sure I don't get caught trespassing. But I can't park here, where is the best place to meet without my car being noticed?"

I pull out the map that Michelle had given me. Que-tip flies over the map I have placed against the steering wheel.

"See that spot there, (as she points with her foot) that is called Stream Walk. You will be coming on the A149 from Kings Lynn. Come up the A149, past the Glucksburg Wood on your right. Take your first right hand turn. Then take the second right hand turn past Folly Convert, if you miss it, that's okay, you can take the third right, Folly Hang. They will both bring you past the Wild Wood, and St. Magdalene's Church. Pull off into the Wild Wood, and walk towards Norwich Gates. Find a place to park in among the trees. Walk along that road, and I will be waiting to take you to the *Stables Tea Room*. The old kennel is just behind there, but it is ready for demolition. They have just been waiting for the go ahead from MI5. The demolition was scheduled a week ago, now that it is a crime scene, all is on hold."

After those directions, I now have a serious migraine. Thank goodness for a GPS. I open the window to let her fly off.

"I better get going, I'll see you later."

"It won't be light yet, is being able to see in the dark one of your gifts?"

"I wish, but don't worry; I have some things I packed that will help, and dark clothes. They won't spot me. I will see you later."

"I thought you had questions you wanted answered?"

"I do, but right now I just need a couple of aspirin and a nap. Bye."

Que-tip leaves with a flutter of her delicate wings. I hope I didn't offend her. I've got to be alone.

I back the car out, leave the crowded parking lot and head south towards, I hope, the town of Kings Lynn. I hold it together for a few minutes at least until I'm on the road, then the tears come. I pull over to the side of the road, turn off the engine, and just let them come.

"Why me?" I knew things were too good to be true. I guess I won't ever get a break. Do they even like me, or did I just imagine they did? I felt a part of a family for the first time in my life. Was it just my imagination? All I ever wanted was a family that would love me, and want me. I was so happy to have found them. I bet that even Aunt Molly knows. What about Mick? Mick is just doing what they ask him, he is just a dog and does whatever he's told. I bet he doesn't even like me.

I'm so busy sobbing that I don't notice a shimmer of light next to me. "What is troubling you dear child?"

"Hi Friar, I'm not very good company right now."

"Perhaps telling me why you are so upset would help."

"Life is just *so unfair!* I was *so happy!* I finally find my family, but they only want to use me. Not love me like I love them, they just want what I can do for them. Why? What did I ever do to them? I saved the land from being taken over by the crooked neighbor, isn't that enough?"

"What makes you think you are being used?"

"I just met a faeire that told me the exciting news that Queen Geraldine has found a relative to help her regain her throne. I guess that relative is me. Now I have to train to battle a magical woman called Morrigan."

"This tells you that your family does not love you?"

"If they did wouldn't they have asked me to help them? Wouldn't they have explained everything to me right away?"

"Perhaps they believed that, meeting eternal beings for the first time was enough for you to come to terms with?

"Could be, I guess."

"Have they ignored your summons?"

"I haven't summoned them."

"You are condemning them without getting their side of the story. Is that fair? Isn't it the Americans that say a man is innocent until proven guilty?"

Hmm, I heard that saying recently. "Yea, but it's not as if they are *human*. Hey, they could have told me the only reason that they had me win the contest to come to Ireland in the first place was to *help them.* I thought that they *wanted me.* I want them. I don't care that two of them are centuries old, they are the only family I have. Even Aunt Molly must have known. The faeire seemed to think that Morrigan could kill me. She thought that I was lucky to get *away* the first time. Am I just a sacrificial lamb to be led to slaughter?"

"If that is true, I wonder why they sent you a mentor."

"Mick?"

"Yes, that was his name. Why would your 'greats' as you call them, go to the trouble of sending you a mentor to aid you?"

"I don't know. My only guess is that I'm meant to put up a struggle, or at least sidetrack Morrigan while they take over, who knows. The one thing that Mick has taught me is to focus, and to let go of fear. He never once mentioned Morrigan. I know for sure that there is *no way* that I will ever be able to take down a Goddess of War. I could focus for days, and it won't help. I will need the British military for that, and maybe even they would have some trouble fighting magic."

"I don't understand why you doubt that you could win a battle with Morrigan. You did help your family save the land, uncover a murderer, and stop a terrorist ring. If someone told you that you would accomplish all that before you went to Ireland, would you have believed them?"

"Of course not, but that's my father's land, and I'm family. Of course, I would help save the family farm."

"Not everyone would."

"So you think I should wait on getting all emotional and ask them what they want from me before I pass judgment?"

"I think that would be wise. You have a lot on your plate right now helping Michelle, and the Royal family. What was that you said about *'Let go and let God'?* I think this may be one of those occasions."

"Okay, I guess you're right. Thank you for listening."

"I will be back in touch soon. Take care my child, enjoy your latest adventure."

Chapter 7

Nighttime Meeting

The room I found is great. A little noisy, since it is directly over a pub, but it's a beautiful, large, light corner room. I did something I never do. But since I told Que-tip I was going to, what the heck. I lay down for a nap.

Heavy fog shrouds the area. A pale green light glows sickly, barely showing me the way. "I'm so cold, can't go on." Then I hear the voices, "We are waiting for you. We need you to help us."

I'm so tired. It feels as if I've been walking for hours. I finally reach a road leading onto the main street of the village. I sense someone behind me, and then...

Lucky for me, an Irish bag piper begins to play, or test his bag. I wake up first fearful with remnants of the nightmare remaining and then thinking that someone has run over a cat. I jump out of bed.

According to the ornate clock on the dresser, it is Two A.M. I get moving to keep my appointment with Que-tip. I shower, and change into the cat burglar outfit I purchased for my last caper in Ireland. Best buy I ever made. I put on a pair of black hiking boots, black jeans, black thick sweater, and a black scarf to cover my hair. Add a large silver bike chain that I hang from my front pocket to the back. That way no one would think my outfit strange. I just look Goth.

Good thing I invested the few extra euros' for the GPS; I could never find my way back at night without it. At the

Palace grounds, I put the GPS volume on mute and slow the car to a crawl. I find the road Que-tip suggested and pull the car into the trees for extra camouflage. Hey, I'm getting good at this detecting stuff. Just knew watching all of those crime shows would pay off someday.

I quietly close the car door, and using my penlight to guide me, open the trunk. I pull out my black backpack, glad I added the extra sweater to the bag to help absorb the noise of the tools banging against each other. When I turn off the light, I look up at the night sky. It's incredible. Away from the city lights, the stars and constellations look as if you could reach out and touch them. One comes right at me..... "Yikes!"

"Be quiet now, noise travels."

"Que-tip, you scared me. I thought you were a falling star and I was about to be bonked on the head."

"I say mate, you have been bonked already. Move on now. The guards are heading this way."

We hurry across the lawn and keep to the shadows. I forgot to ask if there were dogs on patrol. I learned my lesson in Ireland. If dogs are guarding the property then I'm going home.

"Que-tip, are there any guard dogs I have to worry about?"

"Nah, they are too high tech for that. Just bend when I tell you, jump when I tell you, otherwise you will set off the alarms."

We walk for almost an hour. If Que-tip tells me one more time to bend or jump, I will just scream. Next time the dang backpack stays home, it weighs a ton. I guess I shouldn't complain, this is a better workout than all the Wii sports programs put together.

"Jump high now!"

Startled, I jump high but land wrong. My feet fly out from under me. I land on my rump and the back pack. What must have been the rock pick pokes me and I yell, "Ouch."

At the same time I hear a horse nearby whinny loudly. "Sorry Que-tip, thanks for the help. What did you do to the poor horse to have him cry to cover up my noise?"

"What would I do to Fred? I just asked him."

"You can talk to animals?"

"You can't?"

"I don't know. I guess I can talk to Mick, and he's a dog."

"Then you can."

"But, how...."

"Hush now, and watch where you are walking. There is the path to the old kennel straight ahead."

Thank goodness for the bright starlit night. I can just make out the kennel. It's an old stone building about the size of a one car garage. I can see where the rock has tumbled loose from the mortar. No wonder they are tearing it down. The door is crisscrossed with yellow police tape. Now to get in, I duck beneath the tape, check out the lock and pull off my back pack. I carefully remove a plastic card and jimmy the lock.

"How did you learn that?"

"From forgetting my key at home when I went to get the mail. A neighbor showed me how to use a card to open my door if only the top lock caught."

"Top lock?"

"We have three locks on our apartment door, a regular lock, a dead bolt and a metal pole that's welded into the door and floor so that no one can just push our door open."

"And you call that *a home*?"

"It is, or was, we have sublet it for now until we move back to Brooklyn."

"Be quick, the guard is coming."

I open the door as quietly as I can, and shut it just as quietly behind me.

"Que-tip please let me know when it's okay to turn on my flashlight."

"Your what?"

"My torch, I hear critters moving about, and I'd love to turn on a light."

"Okay, the way is clear. He won't be back for another hour."

I turn on my torch and turn to the right. I am looking at a long narrow room with what looks like big wooden toy boxes lined up on one side. I go over and lift one of the lids.

"What are these?"

"This is where the staff feeds and waters the dogs."

She points down and explains, "You can add the feed and water from here on a rainy day and the handler will stay dry. Next to the food and water dish is a bed. They are all under shelter here but if the dogs want, they can run along there (she points to the long dark space beyond the sheltered area) it extends for a dozen meters at least."

"If I climb down there could I get out carrying a cage of puppies?"

"Not likely. There are twenty such runs and each one has a chain link fence separating it from its neighbors. Coming out in broad daylight would draw the attention of the Queen's Guards."

We continue looking around the kennel. I went back to the front room. It looks like my family's cottage in Ireland. It might have been a cottage, and the kennel was added on later. There is a floor to ceiling stone fireplace that has been taped up to warn people not to get too close. A good size room but I wonder what it is used for.

"This place seems really old. Was it a cottage at one time?"

"It was actually a part of the old castle. When Prince Edward purchased it for his young bride, he did an extensive remodel. The section connecting this portion to the old chapel was torn down."

"What was in here most recently?"

"There was a big, old, roll-top desk that sat in the corner over there. On the other side of the fireplace there were grooming tables; beyond them were large, deep stainless steel sinks. All of that was taken to the new kennel."

"So it was on one of those tables that Michelle put the cage which held all of the puppies."

"Sure, and Willie helped her to do it. She is weak, couldn't lift the cage by herself. Or as Lynne says, she wanted to flirt with Willie."

"Your friend thought that Michelle wanted to flirt with Willie? Who are Willie and Lynne?"

"Willie is a grounds man and Lynne is my best bud. She is a little overprotective of Willie. She thinks all female humans are flirting with him. She likes humans, and loves watching them. Willie's eyesight is not as good as it once was, so it is safe for her to hang with him."

"That's great! There is a witness that Michelle placed the cage on the table, and left the building?"

"Don't get your knickers in a twist. We know that she put the cage on the table, and that Willie left right away. No one saw the dogs after that. They just disappeared."

We continue to look around for another hour but I can't see anything of any use. How did I ever think that I could accomplish what others could not? I'm getting ready to leave when I stop to admire the large old stone fireplace.

"How old do you think this building is?"

"I would say it is not too old at all, several hundred years or so."

I smile at Que-tip's view of 'not too old'; I keep forgetting that the Fae think in centuries rather than years. "Since this was part of a much larger 'keep' they might have had a chapel on the property and a priest available for the family."

"Then it must have been before my birth. Bridget, we had better leave now, I think I hear someone coming."

"You're right," I whisper although I don't hear anyone. "Maybe I could return another time, and look some more."

"Possibly!"

"What do you mean, possibly?"

"It is scheduled to be torn down."

"Let me do some more research on-line tonight and we can try again tomorrow."

Then I hear it, the sound of strong, determined steps on the gravel driveway out front.

"Hurry, hide," I whisper, as I move the tape, and take cover in the extra large hearth of the old fireplace. Que-tip flies to my shoulder.

The guard opens the door. He carries a torch that lights up the entire room. As he swings the light around the dark room he shouts "Who goes there, show yourself now."

I know he will soon discover our hiding place. I press back farther into the hearth, and feel the cold stones at my back. I stretch out my right hand to get my balance and the entire back opens, we fall through into complete darkness.

A few of the old bricks fall and I hear the guard speak into his cell. "The old bricks are falling. Must be what I heard, all clear here."

I feel a slight breeze on my face and hear a whispered question from Que-tip, "Where the bloody heck are we?"

The hearth opening swings closed behind us. We are in complete darkness. The dust, mold and damp go to work on my eyes and nose right away. I begin to sneeze. I cover my mouth and squeeze my nose. The sound that escapes is a little strange. Sounds like a very loud squeal.

I hear the guard say to himself "No one is here, just my imagination," as he hurries from the room that makes strange sounds with no one to be seen.

"Que-tip, could you please help me find my torch, I lost it when we fell into this secret room."

"Secret room?"

"Sure, don't teen faeire read murder mysteries? This room must be a major clue. I bet it's a priest hole; perhaps this cottage was once a part of a chapel. During the Reformation, the English priest would grab any signs that he was holding mass and hide. If he was captured he would be imprisoned or killed. Let's check it out."

I find my flashlight and turn it on. The light illuminates a galvanized steel crate with bars. The door is open, I start to shiver. I walk over to the crate and touch the bars. The images of my nightmare return. I can see the puppies and the gloved hand.

"Bridget, what is happening? Why are you crying?"

I take a few deep breaths to shake off the images and am finally able to answer her, "I saw the puppies. We have to find the guy who did this, we must."

"So you are psychometric? Like you have the ability to sense things by touch?"

"I don't think so, maybe? In this case I saw what was happening in a nightmare the other day. I'm just sort of remembering it now. Let's take a look around and see if we can spot anything that they may have left behind. Hopefully something that would give us a clue as to who they are."

The room is small, totally enclosed by stone; I have to shake the feeling that I'm buried alive. I feel sorry for any poor priest that had to hide in here for any length of time. Crawling around is difficult. There is a lot of rubble on the floor but I can't make out what it is. Then we both spot it at the same time, a glove.

"What is that?"

I reach into my pocket for a tissue and use it to pick up the large, black faux leather glove. I have a large zip-lock bag that I got used to carrying when Mick and I went walking in the city. It came in handy as an evidence bag. I had just placed the glove into the bag when there was a loud rumble.

"What's that noise?"

"Sounds like a massive piece of machinery to me, let's get out of here."

I tuck the bag inside my jacket and turn back to the wall that had opened to let us enter. It had shut behind us automatically but there has to be a way to open it from this side.

We look at every stone on that wall for what seems like hours, and then the battery gives out.

"This is not going to happen to me again."

"What do you mean?"

"I learned my lesson in the cave beneath the old fort in Ireland. The Scouts have it right, always be prepared."

I reach into my pocket and begin to tear open a new package of batteries.

"Now why do they have to make everything child proof, I can't get these dang things open."

I'm sitting on the ground Indian style, struggling with the package of batteries, the noise is getting louder.

"You are magic, do something!" cries Que-tip.

"What do you mean, I'm magic. I can't do anything. Heck, I can't even get this dang package open."

"But you are of *Royal* blood, you must be able to do magic."

"Okay, I learned to be grateful for what I have, learned to be positive. Learned how to banish evil faeire and stop worrying about my future. *How on earth does that make me magic?*"

"*You must be.* The old scrolls tell us that you will come and free us. If you are just human, we are all lost."

"I know who can do magic, Mick!" I shout, "I need you Mick. Mick please come as fast as possible. We're in danger! Help!"

We feel the ground rumble and hear stones falling around us.

Chapter 8

Priest Hole

"What is this you are telling me? How on earth did you get into so much trouble in just one week? I spoke with you every day," asks a not too happy Mick.

"Well you asked if I was doing okay and I am, well, sort of. You asked whenever you called.... And how did you do that anyway, speak to me long distance like that? Do you need an extra brain chip or something for long distance, that's just plain *awesome...*"

Mick didn't answer, so I continue explaining. "When you asked if I was seeing the sights, I told you I am. When you asked, where I had been, I told you: Buckingham Palace, St. Paul's Cathedral, the *family home* of the Queen and..."

"True." Mick interrupts, *"Somehow, you neglected to tell me that the reason you were in St. Paul's Cathedral was that you found your English cousin. Who happens to believe that you are destined to join him in stopping its destruction?"*

"Well, it's not like I have done anything about *that* yet."

"But you plan to?" shrieks Mick.

"Hey, don't shriek at my friend," demands Que-tip.

Ignoring her, Mick continues, *"You also neglected to mention, this young lady here, a teenage hoodlum if ever I saw one."*

"Hey watch it buddy, I may be small, but I have friends in high places."

Que-tip flies a few inches above Mick's eyes. Her little body shaking as she confronts a dog a hundred times her size. She is pointing her finger at him, and the large head of white, cotton ball looking hair, is shaking from side to side.

"Oh, pardon me, Miss Ear Wax is it? How did you talk Bridget into this scheme that has her locked in an ancient priest hole? A priest hole, that is about to be knocked down by a bloody wrecking ball."

"Mick, I never said she talked me into it, if you would only listen. Practice what you have been teaching me, okay? Take a deep breath. Que-tip is a teenage faeire, which of course, is why she can hear you speak. Que-tip is not affected by Morrigan, no one, under what she calls, the age of reasoning... whatever that is, is affected. She is going to help me take down Morrigan. But before she does, she wants me to come and speak with her group."

"Help you do what?"

"Yeah, like you don't know. When were you and my old Greats going to let me in on the game plan? Noooo, I have to learn it from a stranger. I shouldn't be speaking with you, but I do need your help in getting out of here, and *like soon* please. I can hear that wrecking ball. It's getting closer."

I could see that Mick is ready to argue some more, so I interrupt before he gets going again.

"It was Friar Xavier who actually got me here. Well he and Michelle. Except Michelle cannot see the Friar since he's the ghost who watches over the royal family. Funny how I can see him, I guess I can do all sorts of things I don't know about yet." I hear a low doggie growl and talk a little faster.

"Well, you see the Queen raises Corgi's, and she has bred them with Dachshunds. Now she is the proud owner of a new breed called Dorgis. Except someone has dog napped the puppies! Michelle was caring for them, and she is from France.

"The papers are blaming the French people. *It's a mess*. So I'm just investigating. Then Que-tip and I discovered this place, and we got locked in."

The sound of large machinery is almost on top of us. Large pieces of rock begin to follow the dirt and chunks of mortar that have been coming down.

"Mick, can you get us out......like *now*!" I shout.

I close my eyes and cover my face to stop inhaling the dust. I feel like I'm back in the wind tunnel ride at Coney Island. My feet no longer touch the ground. I'm being tossed around. I uncover my eyes but can't see anything except a dense fog with what looks like Christmas lights flickering. Finally it stops and I'm able to feel grass under me. I look around and realize that I'm lying next to my rental car.

"Que-tip, where are you? Are you okay?"

"What a trip, thank you my....Ah, Mick was it?"

"Nothing you could not have done yourself."

"What does he mean; could you have gotten us out of there?"

"I could have left anytime. But what type of a friend would I be if I left you behind?"

"Thank you Que-tip, and thank you Mick. Whew that was a trip. Now I have to get to Scotland Yard and give them the evidence we found."

"Why not turn it over to the constable here?"

"Que-tip, if I go to someone local then they may arrest me for breaking in on a crime scene.

"You are taking it to the Yard for an opportunity to visit with the inspector that arrested that felon from Ireland!"

"Mick, don't sound so grumpy. Charlie is a smart cop and he knows me. Besides what's wrong with using this as an opportunity to meet up with Charlie again? He did say he would show me around London if I ever made the trip over here."

"So who is Charlie?"

"He's a detective inspector that is now assigned to the Criminal Investigation Department or the CID. His office is in the New Scotland Yard. I have his card. I'll call him and hopefully he can see us right away."

We all pile into the car for the trip to London. Que-tip is looking in the rearview mirror and dusting herself off.

"Bridget, I think you may wish to stop at your flat for a quick dust off."

I look down at my black outfit that is now white with dust.

"You think?"

We all laugh and head to Battersea.

We luck out and find a parking place right in front of the Hard Rock Café. It is not a quiet out of the way place but it was Que-tip's choice. She looked so excited about getting a chance to go. I figure Charlie could put up with a little noise.

We timed this meeting just right. There are no lines in front of the restaurant but I notice the gift shop next door is packed. When I open the large impressive door, we are hit with sound. Elvis is singing Jailhouse Rock and there are more than a hundred people from various cultures all talking at once.

I wish I could see the look on Que-tip's face as she takes in the décor. I can feel her excitement from the flutter of her wings against my neck.

"I have to get a closer look." Que-tip informs me as she flies up towards the ceiling. When I look where she is headed, I have to laugh out loud; there are guitars, drums and all sorts of things up there to amuse her. I hope she enjoys herself.

Charlie came over; he looks up to see what I am laughing at and sees the old time memorabilia on the ceiling and smiles.

"It's a fun place."

"Let's get a seat."

A waitress in a poodle skirt straight from the fifties shows us to a booth in the back. It is a little quieter. The menu is good and we both order cheeseburgers. While we wait for the food we both look around at all of the great signed photographs, records, costumes and instruments. When the food arrives, I realize that I'm starving. It must be all of the excitement.

"Bridget it is grand to see you again, you mentioned you had some evidence to give me."

I notice Charlie has the most dreamy eyes but he had that 'all business' look about him now that he finished his meal. I reluctantly put down my burger and reach into my handbag for the glove securely sealed in the zip-lock plastic bag. I explain about meeting Michelle, leaving out Friar Xavier of course, my visit to the old kennel, finding the priest hole and barely getting out in time.

"You entered a building that had been posted?"

Charlie's eyes were no longer dreamy, they show his anger and concern for my safety. Heck, I thought meeting in a fun restaurant would soften this lecture part of the conversation.

To get him focused on problem solving, I suggest, "You can still recover the crate and perhaps dust that for fingerprints. It may be a little squished but it was a high quality steel crate, it should still be recognizable."

He takes out his cell and asks to be connected to the Sandringham Garda. As I listen to his side of the conversation I finish my burger.

He completes his call, reaches into his pocket and throws twenty euro on the table.

"I have no idea how I am going to explain all of this without bringing you into it but I will try. Are you staying at the flat in Battersea?"

"Yes. Will you let me know as soon as you find out anything?"

"Okay, but you must promise to leave the detecting to CID. You are a tourist, go see the sights."

"I have, really I can't get into any trouble. There is no more that I can think of to do to find the puppies. It's all in your hands now. I'm going to meet my cousin tonight and have a nice family dinner."

He looks me over with a piercing look that I often get from Mick. "I had better get to it. I will call you in a few days."

He gets up and walks to the front door as Que-tip flies down to my shoulder.

"*He did not look very pleased that we solved his case for him.*"

"He hasn't caught them yet, but he will. Want to have something to eat?"

Que-tip looks at my burger and shutters. "*No thank you but I would like to have a Coke.*"

I place a to-go order with the waitress for a double hamburger for Mick and a small milkshake I would share with Que-tip. No Coke for her, that's all I need, a crazed faeire on a caffeine high. We all head back to the flat for a well deserved nap.

Chapter 9

London Pub

I wake up with a start and jump out of bed. I just know I'm late for work and rush to the bathroom. I trip over a chair and finally wake up enough to realize it's the phone ringing and not the alarm clock.

It isn't dark outside; I haven't slept very long.

"Hello"

"Is this Bridget?"

"Yes, who's calling?"

"This is your cousin Peter."

"Hi, how are you doing?"

"I am grand, thank you. I wish to speak with you. Do you have time to meet up?"

"I would love to meet you. Would you like to come to Battersea? I could make us some dinner."

"That would be grand. What time would work for you?"

I quickly open my cell phone to check the time. It's only two p.m. I'd only slept an hour, no wonder I feel horrible. Thinking quickly, I have to go grocery shopping, take another shower to wake up, cook. Ah the heck with it.

"Why don't we meet somewhere, it might be easier."

"There is a pub called the Woodman on High Street, do you know of it? It has great sharers." "Sharers?"

"Yes, they are appetizers. I went to a party there and it is a good spot. Would that be acceptable, or would you prefer another place?"

"No, that will be fine. I have a GPS, I'll find it. Will parking be a problem?"

"Shouldn't be if we get there early. Say 5 p.m., would that work for you?"

Good, he is as anxious to meet me as I am to meet him. I wish I knew how I could help, hopefully I'll think of something.

"That'll be great. I'll see you there."

As he said good-bye and hung up the phone, I realize I have no idea what to wear. I will go for dressy casual; a girl can never go wrong with classy. I gather up my robe and head for the shower. Maybe I will think clearer after a hot shower.

"I am glad you are going to meet him at a pub. I loved the Hard Rock Café. Will this one be as grand?"

"Oh no you don't, you and Mick stay here and rest. I'll be fine. This is just a meeting with my cousin. No big deal." I hurry into the shower over their protests.

"Mick you cannot come in with me. I'm not going to make believe that I'm blind so that you would be welcomed. You insisted on coming so you will just have to wait in the car."

"Ms. Ear Wax gets to come with you."

Before Que-tip could start in on Mick, I open the car door. "I've left all of the windows down in case you want to use a tree, but please don't leave the car unless you really need to. I would hate to have a rental stolen."

I think I'm lucky I can't make out the language Mick replied in. One of these days I really need to learn Gaelic.

"What does your cousin look like?"

"A lot like my dad. I hope the place is not crowded."

As soon as my eyes adjust to the dark interior, I spot him. I let out a gasp and heard from both Mick and Quetip.

"What is wrong…?"

"I am coming in…."

"No, please you two, everything's okay. It's just a flash back about my dad. He died when I was young but I still think of him a lot."

Peter is leaning against a bar stool with his back to the bar, intently watching the front door. I am flooded with emotions and some negative memories of dad and bars. I put a stop to the negatives and thought about how blessed I am to have family.

I slowly walk towards him and he meets me half way.

"Hi Bridget, I forgot to tell you that you are the spitting image of your Aunt Winnie, did you know that, gave me a start for a moment."

"You are the spitting image of my dad."

"Let's have a seat at one of the booths in back. We have a great deal to talk about."

A waitress came over and we order a "sharer" and tea. I'm happy to see that he's not a heavy drinker.

"How have you been amusing yourself?"

I tell Peter of all the sights I've seen and how much I love his city. I told him of my drive to Norfolk and stay at

Kings Lynn and that I have fallen in love with the English countryside. He is quiet and we find we are comfortable enough to be silent with each other.

"I forgot to ask about your latest case. Is everything okay?"

"I was locating a missing child. I felt I should have been working on St. Paul's but I could not say no to the mom."

"When I visited St. Paul's I saw a chapel dedicated to the American soldier, it's beautiful. There was also a painting there that gave me the shivers."

"I know the one you are referring to, I get the same reaction. St. Paul's Cathedral became an inspiration to the British people during the Second World War. It miraculously escaped major bomb damage whilst buildings in the surrounding areas were reduced to rubble. Do you know that a total of 28 bombs landed on St. Paul's during the Blitz? It only survived because of the volunteers that made up the St. Paul's Watch. Images of St. Paul's framed by the smoke and fire caused by the bombing became a symbol of our nation's indomitable spirit."

"So if you want to hurt the people of England, what better way than to destroy someplace that means so much?"

"Exactly."

"I don't understand. What brings people to want to destroy such a wonderful, historic building? It just doesn't make sense to me."

"The way I see it, they must hate what the church stands for. People teach their kids to hate; it is not something we are born with. I had a teacher once who really helped to open my eyes. Her lecture that day was entitled *'Believe in something, or fall for anything.'*

"She asked us to fold a sheet of paper in three columns. On the first column, she had us write important subject headers, such as: religion, wealth, environment etc. On the second column we were asked to write what *we believed* on the subject. We were asked not to think about it, just write down our beliefs. No one would see this paper; it was just for *our benefit.* On the third column, we were asked to look at all of the answers we wrote in column two and really think about when we first heard that comment, thought, whatever.

"I realized then that I had few thoughts of my own; they were mostly from my parents, friends, neighbors, or the newspapers. For example with the topic of global warming, I wrote *'another way the government wants to take our money'.* Can you believe it? Where did that come from? When I thought about it, it was from a loud cranky neighbor, who no one liked, but he was well read, and we listened to his opinion, and believed him. It was easier to take on someone else's belief than do the research to find out the facts.

"After that class I found myself in the library checking out the stories on global warming, the war in the middle east, the holocaust, and heck even the crusades so I might begin to understand religion, just about *everything* I had an opinion on. I wanted it to be *my* opinion. Not someone else's. Hey I even got angry that *I allowed others to tell me how to believe* without checking out the facts for myself.

"The people who want to blow up St. Paul's never had a teacher who asked them to stop and think *why* they believe what they do. They don't know if it is from a cranky neighbor. They are just taught to hate, and go blindly into that hate. If someone is a different color, different size or different race or different religion, why would you use *your energy* to hate them? I could see not liking a person who did *you* wrong, but a whole race or group of people? It just does not make sense to me."

"I agree it doesn't make sense to me either."

"Sorry for sounding like I am on a soapbox. That teacher really made a difference in my life. The class discussed their thoughts on the subject of beliefs later and several of the foreign students got misty eyed when they realized what the word freedom really means. We are free to believe what we want, not what others tell us to believe. That little exercise really impacted all of us big time."

"That's awesome, what a great teacher."

"She was."

Peter lifts his glass to take a long drink and I notice that he is showing the strain he's under. The other night I thought he was just tired from his trip. He has dark circles under his eyes and a haunted look. I think his nightmares must be coming often and are really bad. He's young but he looks tired and worn out. Are these 'gifts' worth it? I enjoy helping others as Peter said he did, but at what price to us?

I look up and Que-tip has finished her investigation of the sports channel and is sprinkling dust and blowing it at Peter. For a moment I was going to ask her what she was doing but thought I would wait and see. At first nothing happened. Then out of nowhere a lively breeze whirled around us both, a breeze that felt full of hope and humor. She pulls at her top, straightens her shoulders and pats her hairdo, as if she just gave herself a pat on the back for a job well done.

Peter looks at me and smiles. He looks so much better. It's as if he has some of his strength and confidence back.

"Bridget you have a beautiful smile. What has you in such a fine humor?"

I silently thank my faeire friend. "Just my new friend Que-tip, she's a teen faeire." I explain how I met Que-tip and that she has told me what she thinks my destiny is.

"You are to stop the Goddess of War! They must be bonkers, and how are you supposed to do that?"

"I guess that's what all of this is leading up to. I'm slowly but surely learning. When I accept all of the gifts I have been given, I will be able to do anything, so they say. It's still very hard to wrap my mind around."

"I can understand that feeling, and I only have the one gift. I do have to admit that there is no better feeling in the world than the one you get when you know you have helped someone in need."

"Speaking of need, how are we doing with St. Paul's, any leads?"

"No luck on a map but one bloke told me to go to the British Legion. It is located not far from St. Paul's. There are fellows that grew up in that neighborhood. Some had dad's who were part of the St. Paul's watch during the war. They may know much more than anyone else does."

"Sounds like a plan, when do we go?"

"As soon as we finish eating, okay to take your car? I came over by tube."

"Sure, you'll just have to put up with Mick and Que-tip."

"No problem. Wish I could communicate with them as you do."

"You might be able to. It depends on Mick's mood. Although the way they have been squabbling, you may regret your wish to hear them."

Chapter 10

British Legion

We find a parking place on a beautiful, old side road. Brick townhouses and gardens with wrought iron fencing line the street. Not a high class neighborhood, but one that shows the people care. It's well maintained with no graffiti, and no gates on the doors or windows. This is a community where the neighbors watch out for one another.

The building where the British Legion is located is very different from the American Legion buildings I've seen back home. This is not a plain square building in the center of a parking lot. The British Legion is located on the ground floor of a brownstone, three story walk-up. It looks as if it is part of the neighborhood. You enter from street level. The design is slightly different from its neighbors. No steps leading up to the second floor from the street, so all stairs must be on the inside.

We walk into a long narrow room. On the left, next to the door is a small stage. A tall, distinguished, older woman with jet black hair is singing and playing the piano. The furniture looks like what you would expect to find in a pub. Beautiful old wood, leather chairs and tables. Some tables against the wall are set to seat two or four. A few toward the back are joined together to seat six to a dozen patrons at a time. At the back of the room is a small bar. Over the bar is a large mirror. Now that's clever. The mirror shows the bartender who's coming in, even when he has his back to the door.

Peter pulls out a chair at the table for twelve, "Have a seat here a second and I will speak with the barkeep."

A few minutes later a number of men who look like they are in their eighties come over to sit with me. I smile but don't know what to say. Peter comes back with a couple of pitchers of beer and I notice the guys come over with glasses in hand.

"Drink up lads, my cousin wants to thank you for the grand chapel that is dedicated to the American soldier. There is plenty more where this came from, enjoy."

Peter set a glass with dark liquor topped with foam in front of me. I hope it isn't Guinness. I tried a sip in Ireland, and a sip was enough. I pick it up and sniff, thankfully its root beer. After a few dozen comments of, 'Brilliant', 'Welcome Miss', I begin to talk about St. Paul's, the chapel and the painting of St. Paul's during the blitz.

Six men stay sitting with us. They tell us stories of families who survived and the losses they endured, the rebuilding of a city. It is all incredible; I could have stayed and listened to them for hours. Then Peter asks, "Was there a bomb shelter around that you used when Gerry was coming?"

All are silent, deep in thought. One fellow with a mass of white hair that helps to highlight his sky blue eyes, removes his pipe and calls out, "Hey Maggie, me girl, come over, join us for a pint, a gift from the good lady here."

I turn to see who George is speaking with and notice a dark shadow rise from a seat against the wall. She'd been hidden from view by the stage. There is only room for one chair and no table where she was sitting. I have a strong feeling that Maggie is a woman who prefers her own company but likes the noise of people around.

It's very warm in the Legion Hall but Maggie is wearing a heavy black wool coat with a large, faded, red, silk flower. Her bright orange wig is held on with a bright green satin ribbon covered with more silk flowers. She walks very slowly and sits in a chair behind George.

"Please join us Maggie, would you like something to drink?"

All I get is a shake of her head as she seemed to duck behind George, as if for protection. Wow, I wonder what her life was like, what stories she could tell. George repeats Peter's question to Maggie but I can't hear what her answer is.

George turns to Peter, "Maggie and her family took cover in the Underground at Foster Lane. Ain't there now, been shut up tight for years."

"Why would they close a tube station in this area, don't they need all they can use?"

"As if one can understand anything the government does these days. Could be ready to fall in?"

They all pipe in then with one of the major entertainments in any bar, sharing opinions, no matter how crazy. We hear everything from it being unsafe, haunted, to government cutbacks. After we got directions to Foster Lane, we get up to leave. Peter announces that the tab is still open for anyone to enjoy a pint or two on the Yanks. We leave the building and I'm glad to breathe fresh air. It's a good thing that most public places have a no smoking ban. That was a lot of smoke for one small place.

"I'm glad Que-tip returned to the car the moment we opened the door to the Legion Hall. The smoke could not be healthy for anyone, especially one her size," Peter comments as if reading my thoughts.

"Okay if we walk to Foster Lane, Mick could use a walk."

"Sure, it isn't far from here." Peter holds a GPS that shows a map of the area that includes all the current Underground stations and bus routes. "Bridget, could you take a look at this, and tell me what you make of it?" He asks. "Do you see anything unusual?"

"I see Foster Lane, but the station is almost a mile away from here at Newgate Street. Why make everyone walk that far when Foster Lane is so much closer. That doesn't make sense to me."

"Keep looking!" Peter says as he uses a stylus to click on the arrows to move the screen in an easterly direction.

"Oh no! If there's a deserted tunnel, it may go underneath not only St. Paul's, but Fleet Street, and the Exchange. They are right near one another. They may be planning to take down all three!"

"That would also give us a reason why it has been abandoned. A tunnel directly under the Exchange would be a threat to the country's economic structure."

"Let's find it. Mick and Que-tip, we need your help with this; the opening has been shut down a long time. No telling where it is."

"Que-tip, stay with Bridget, I can sniff it out."

Que-tip flies to her spot on my shoulder, and I release Mick from the leash.

"You just want an excuse to run after being stuck in the car. Whatever you do, please don't get picked up by the dog catcher, you still don't have a license."

I hear a growl, and a laugh from Peter as Mick swiftly disappears around the corner.

"Was that growling a way of communicating with you?"

"Yes, he does that often when I hurt his doggie pride. He's a character, but he'll help us find the station now that we have some idea where to look."

We walk about ten blocks when we turn a corner to a much older section of store fronts, and dirty alleys. I walk past a grocer with an old faded awning. There are large wooden boxes filled with fruit that have seen better days. Most of it is spotted and the flies have gathered. Not a great advertisement.

I smell fresh bread. I follow the smell and find a baker half way down an alley. No storefront, they must sell to the larger stores, and use this warehouse for a base. The alley is typical of those in New York. Clothes-lines hang between the buildings. They are strung with blankets, and sheets hung to dry.

We can hear music playing, some kind of a high whining instrument. I'm about to turn around, and leave the alley when I hear Mick, *"Come to the end of the alley. You will see a large wooden door. It looks like it leads to another warehouse, but as soon as you get inside you will see the entrance to the tube."*

We rush to the end of the alley to join Mick. It is starting to get dark. I'm happy that Peter remembered to bring a flashlight.

Somehow Mick opened a very large lock, and removed the chain that had been wrapped around a metal pole. It is so rusted it must not have been opened for years. Peter is quiet as we tiptoe into the old station. He moves ahead, which is fine with me since he gets to knock down all of the cobwebs. He has put on a sweatshirt jacket with hood, and is now wearing gloves. Why didn't I think to grab my tool kit, it might've come in handy.

To keep my mind off any possible creepy crawlies, I look around at the entrance that appears to be the same size as the larger tube stations like Paddington.

We are walking on a floor of beautiful old tile, about the size of nickels, and cut octagonal. I think if they were cleaned up they would be bright yellow color with black grout. The walls have the standard large white subway tile we have at home, but the name of the station is in a repeat of the floor tile.

Peter swept the station with his light. I can make out ticket booths that are shrouded in cobwebs and many years of dust that the faint breeze from the open door is stirring around.

"This does not make sense. It looks as if we are the first people here in a long time. But in my vision I have seen three men and a track. Could there be another entrance?"

"Must be if you think your vision is happening now and not in the future. We are the first to come into this entrance in quite awhile. See how thick the dust is and no footprints."

"Let's keep looking, I am going down to the platform, do you want to stay here? Those stairs may not be safe."

"You have the only light, I'm going with you."

"*Bridget?*"

"Don't worry Mick, I'll be okay, where are you?"

"*Peter can you hear me?*"

"Yes, I can. That is brilliant."

I could hear the awe in Peter's voice. Being an old hat at magic, a talking dog didn't seem to faze him a bit.

"*Both of you hug the wall on the way down. The railing is too frail to hold for much longer.*"

Peter's light is no help at all. I can see in front of him but not in front of where I'm stepping. I am slowly going down a step at a time, trying not to touch the old wall that gave off a horrible smell of mold and mildew. Peter stops. The light reaches out faint fingers of light all around. I can make out the walls that contain shreds of old advertisements, half torn away and faded with time. One said, '*Careless Talk Costs Lives,*' telling us when the station was closed. Maybe it was hit by a bomb during the war.

"Stay here, I'll check the track."

"Wait I'll..."

There is blackness and silence. I don't know how long it'll last but I have to make the most of it. I can hear my breath and feel my heart race. A low moaning whimper escapes me. Someone else is in the tunnel; he's making scraping sounds as he moves down the tracks. The next station can't be more than two minutes away, could it? I keep moving. I can see signal lights ahead. Doesn't that mean a station was near or was it a junction? Beside the signal lights there is a small niche in the wall.

On the floor I can make out some tools, discarded or left deliberately for the next man on the next job. I bend over and find I'm blocking the weak light. I can hear the scraping noise coming closer. I run my fingers over the tools and grasp what feels like a pipe or a wrench. It's heavy, about a foot long. At least I now have something to defend myself with. He's close now. I turn to run; his large arm comes around my throat. He drops his light. I can see my shadow on the tunnel wall. I am wearing a dress. That is not me.

Blackness, he's carrying a light in his left hand and in its glow I can see a man gazing back at me. He's tall and wearing an exotic outfit. He looks familiar. He has heavy black eyebrows that are not completely covered by the thick, black rimmed glasses. He smiles and I almost return his smile until I notice that in his right hand he is holding a large black gun pointed directly at me.

My feet are frozen in place, I open my mouth to yell for Mick but no sound comes. I can't think. A flash of light, a muffled pop, I look down at my chest, where there had once been a clean, crisp white shirt, there is blood...

"Bridget, are you okay?"

"I'm..." I press my hand against my chest, no blood. What the heck? I move my hand to the wall to help me to sit up and my blood freezes. *I can feel it all at once, the pain, the fear of dying, the horrible loss of those killed. I am seeing and feeling the past and perhaps my future.*

With a forceful nudge of his head, Mick pushes my hand away from the wall.

"Thank you Mick."

"Thank Que-tip there; she is the one who told me you now have the gift of Psychometry."

"What is Psychometry?" asks a worried looking Peter.

"It's a form of extra-sensory perception. Mick has taught me that most objects have an energy field that transfers knowledge regarding that object's history."

"Brilliant!"

"Can be, once I learn to control it, right now I have to be careful touching things that may give off negative imprints."

"Would have been nice to know that your gifts are increasing," grumbled Mick.

"Yea, I meant to mention that."

"What happened? Are you okay?"

I feel like I was pushed but there's no one else here. Mick or Que-tip would have sensed them, wouldn't they?

"Just missed my step and fell, must have knocked my head on the wall. Was I out for long?"

"Out?"

"You know, passed out. I had the strangest dream."

"Bridget, you were just dazed for a second."

I look at the worried faces around me, "Sorry about that. Must be the history I was picking up from the wall. Let's get onto the track and see where it leads."

Peter reaches out and I grasp his hand. I get up quickly and feel dizzy. I take one step and yelp. "Darn, I think I sprained my ankle."

"You need that iced and bandaged right away. You all stay here. I will get the car."

He turns to leave and I call out, "Peter, I'm okay, don't worry."

"I am not worried, didn't you ever hear that we English are cool and under control at all times?"

"Sure, but don't you think you may need the car keys?"

"Right you are. Here keep the torch, I will be okay. Mick, see that she stays put."

I look at Que-tip and grumble, "Men are all the same aren't they?"

"You can say that again."

"*What do you two mean by that?*"

"Rather than admit he is upset or worried about me, he gets bossy and rushes to do something away from here."

"A woman would handle the situation a little differently. If he was hurt, I would first make sure he was comfortable, maybe assist him to street level rather than leave him here in the dark and dirt."

"*But he left you the torch?*"

Que-tip and I look at each other and smile. Mick just shakes his head. I lean against the post, refusing to sit on the floor again. I gently flex my leg, testing to see if pain shouts the news of broken bones or torn muscles. No, it is bruised, but aside from the throb I seem okay. I notice the dirt on my outfit.

"I must look a mess, best that he gets the car. I don't want to walk ten blocks looking like this."

Okay, it's not the wall that brought the vision of my rush thru the tunnel. I've seen that guy before, but where? Was the vision showing me I was going to be shot? What the heck was that? That had better not be a sign of what was to come.

"Hey guys, I think we need more help on this."

"Who, we can't go to the Inspector. He will not believe this 'intuition' of Peter's."

"You're right Mick; the normal avenue is closed for now. Que-tip, could you get a message to Friar Xavier?"

"Sure."

"Please show him where I live and meet us there. I've a couple of questions for him. Besides, I want to know if they've found the dog-nappers yet."

With a twirl of her little body, she's off.

I point the light along the track to my left and it is barricaded at the tunnel's mouth. They were definitely not being used in that direction. I point the light along the track to my right. I can make out the walls of the tunnel a good distance from where I'm standing. They are black with soot and age.

"Mick, did you check out the tracks?"

"I did, I went along them for a bit of a way. I had just come to a fork where two tracks meet up when I heard you cry out."

"Were there any signs of recent activity or people?"

"I could not smell the presence of people but with the other smells of oil and debris, it is hard to tell if anyone has passed this way recently."

"Did you reach another station?"

"I saw signal lights ahead. I think there may be another station a kilometer from where I turned back."

"We have to know for sure. Mick, do you know of any magic that will heal my ankle so that I can jump down on the track and check it out myself?"

Mick gave me a puzzled, questioning look and shakes his head. *"Bridget, what is needed is for you to rest. Stay out of trouble, study the books I have given you and learn all the magic that you may be capable of."*

"Thank you Doctor Mick. That does not help. Didn't you hear Peter; we need to help him now."

"You need to rest and ice your ankle. Then you will be okay in a day or two."

"Mick, I don't have a day or two."

"There now, calm down. We will help him. Go over to the crate and sit down. You should not be standing."

Mick walked a few feet to a large crate that I'd not noticed before. It looked like the wooden box that the fruit vendor had his oranges in. It looks solid enough. I hop over and sit down.

"Funny I didn't see this here before."

Mick ignores me and continues, *"This must be another test that your ancestors set in your path for you to bring out more of your gifts. When this is over we do need to discuss the upcoming battle with Morrigan. I wish you had not heard about it the way that you did. We meant no harm keeping it from you. We did not give your inner strength enough credit. We thought you would feel overwhelmed and head back to America."*

"I want to. I don't know how I'm going to help. I don't like what's happening to Que-tip's family and friends, no mind the rest of the world. Morrigan has to be stopped. Que-tip said it was a miracle that I escaped her wrath in the caves of Ireland. How did I do that?

"I have spoken with your ancestors and they believe that you automatically raised a protective shield."

"Wow, like a super hero! Except those rocks she bombarded me with still hurt, did I do it wrong?"

"We should be practicing how to bring your shield forth when needed."

"Okay with me, I may need it for more than just Morrigan. Can it protect me from bullets?"

"Only if your shield is in place in time. I am sorry to say the wrath of Morrigan is stronger than bullets."

"Can you tell me how to set it in place now while we are waiting?"

"Close your eyes and try to still and calm your mind as I have taught you. Stillness is not easy to bring forth with the pain you are experiencing from your ankle. It will help if you breathe slowly and deeply..."

Back at the flat I look around at the four anxious faces staring at me. "Peter, I forgot to tell you that I invited another guest to help us. One person that you may not be able to see, his name is Friar Xavier. He is the spiritual guardian to the Royal family.

Peter looks to his left, "Pleased to meet you Friar," and holds out his hand.

I nod to Peter that the Friar is on his right. "That's okay Peter, the Friar is not used to shaking hands."

I explain to the Friar about Peter and his visions, and how important it is to get protection for the Cathedral. "Friar, does the Queen attend service at St. Paul's?"

"On occasion she does."

"Do you know of any occasion she may be attending there in the near future?"

"No Bridget, it cannot be. I thought we decided that St. Paul's would be destroyed for shock value."

"Sorry Peter but I had a vision that leads me to believe killing the Queen is part of the whole picture."

"What vision," asked four voices at once?

I explain what really happened in the tube station. Of course leaving out the part where I'm shot. "I believe I may have seen the man in the tunnel in a recent picture. He is standing with the Royal family."

Friar sits on the edge of my bed, missing my foot by inches. Wringing his hands and shaking his head. "Here I thought we were on the way to solving one mystery, and now we are looking for a would-be assassin. This is too much for one spirit."

We talk over all of the angles and I notice Peter slumping in his chair, and ready to fall asleep.

"Peter, please go home and rest. You can take the car. I'll be okay, how *can* I get into any trouble with three babysitters?"

"Okay, only if you promise to rest yourself. I will call you tomorrow. Is there anything else I can get you?"

I am lying on my bed with my foot on two fluffy pillows. Next to me is the TV clicker, a bottle of Coke, a pitcher of water, today's paper, a stack of magazines, Mick, Que-tip and Friar Xavier.

"No Peter, I'm sure I won't need anything else for the next twenty-four hours. Please go home and rest."

"Goodnight then."

"Goodnight."

"I'll lock the door behind me."

"Thank you. Goodnight."

When I hear the door close, I attempt to get up, and then hear Mick growl, and Que-tip say, "No."

"Hey guys, give me a break will ya? I have to go to the bathroom."

I am able to stand, but walking or hopping is a hassle. I feel a cold arm holding me, "Thank you Friar, I'm okay, really. You could do me a big favor and go check on what dates the Queen is expected to attend St. Paul's.

"I would also like the names of those attending. Perhaps I can research them on Google. Could you also check on Michelle? I'm so worried about her. I need to know if they found the Dorgis. I bet the Queen is worried sick."

"Oh goodness, Her Majesty, of course, I will check on her right off, and let you know her itinerary straight away."

I almost fell again when the Friar suddenly left, but Mick had somehow moved a chair under me and I sit down quickly.

"That was fast thinking, I would like to see what excuse you use to get rid of Que-tip."

"Perhaps there is a way to make a dog disappear."

"Stop it you two. I'm going to take a quick shower, and go to bed, so both of you, put a sock in it now."

I stand, and limp into the bathroom, trying to look as dignified as I can. I hear Que-tip and Mick discussing what they need to do with socks and chuckle.

Interlude

Gift of Psychometry

In the protection of the harbor, the water is smooth and glistening. Mick stretches his arms towards the sky and lifts his face to the sun. He needs the calming influence of sun and water. The heat feels warm and comforting on his bare skin. Its majestic warmth cocooning him in the peace and quiet he craved.

He feels Padraig's presence, but does not acknowledge his old friend. They stay silent, enjoying the morning sun beaming down on the water, watching the myriad of birds as they plunge into the sea to fish, the seals, as they occasionally poke their heads up or rest on their backs.

"You are troubled?"

"In so many ways, I cannot begin to tell you."

"Please try, I am your friend. I am here to assist you in any way I can."

How do I begin to explain? The intimate connection, so deep, so strong, shook him. Her loving warmth surrounds him.

Instead he says, "Bridget has uncovered another gift, that of Psychometry. Que-tip, the faeire, informed me that this is so. She suffered a slight injury that I could not prevent. What can I tell you, it unmanned me. There is an energy building between us. I cannot bear her to suffer, if I am unable to prevent Morrigan..."

"Bridget is the strong, self-confident woman we knew her to be. She is intelligent. She is gifted. She will be able to stop Morrigan. You must believe this. You, most of all, must believe that she can do this. You know that you must not begin to doubt, to allow thoughts of her failing to enter your mind. You must begin to imagine, as we are, her total success."

They watch the sea, lost in thought.

"I am certain that Bridget also has deep feelings for you..."

"As a dog!"

"As a friend and companion, one she would lay down her life for. That is all you can ask of her. She must concentrate her strength on learning the skills she will need to defeat Morrigan."

"I will lay down my life for her. She has given me a gift beyond measure."

"What is that my young lord?"

"To feel loved and to be able to love in return."

Chapter 11

Cupcakes

"Come in Peter. I'm out back in the garden."

Peter looks much better this morning. I think finding the tunnel entrance helped him feel as though he's getting closer to solving this case of his. Great, he's carrying a bakery box, good man.

"Can I get you a cup of tea, the kettle is still hot?"

"You stay sitting, I will help myself. Would you like a cup? I brought us some cupcakes from the Hummingbird Bakery. I heard that they are famous for American style baked goods and thought you might like some."

"Yes please, I would love one." I hear a low growl. "Don't worry Mick, I'll share with you."

The morning is glorious, the fog has burned off and it is now bright and sunny. I lay back in the lounge chair and enjoy the early morning sounds. Peter carries out a tray with his tea cup and a fresh hot pot of tea for both of us. I pour my now cool tea in Mick's bowl, and add some into a thimble I picked up for Que-tip.

"Thank you for the cupcakes, I don't believe I ever had a cupcake that tastes like a cinnamon bun before, this is wonderful."

"It is my pleasure. How are you feeling? You do look much better."

"I have not been allowed to do much except rest and relax. My ankle feels much better. I'm sure I can walk on it with no problem now."

I take one of the least sugary looking baked goods from the box for Mick and Que-tip to share.

"Bridget, you look happy. Do you have some good news?"

"I actually have some great news. I think I know who is behind this attack."

"How? Did you call the yard?"

"No, not yet. Last night I mentioned the guy in my vision..."

Peter nods, his cupcake all but forgotten, half way to his mouth.

"I'd seen him someplace, but couldn't remember where. I've only been here at the house, and playing tourist. I took another look at all of the magazines and newspapers that are stacked for recycle, and then I found it."

"Who is he?"

"I think it might be Prince Oama Hassin, it looks a lot like him."

"Who?"

"Prince Oama is the older brother that had to stay at home with the family, and be trained to take over the country as the future Amir. I think he plans on taking out the Queen, and the Cathedral. My guess is that he doesn't like the English, has a grudge against this country and his brother."

"Who is the brother?"

"Prince Ammed Hassin, he's younger by a few years. He was born in his country, and then sent, when he was a young kid, to boarding schools in England. He sounds like he loves all things English. Including the women... He is marrying an Englishwoman."

"Why were they in the news?"

"The article on 'The Royals' highlighted the upcoming wedding. The bride is a minor English royal, the Queen is her Godmother. The Queen and many of the royal families plan to attend. The young Prince wants to strengthen ties between his small country and the English people. He plans to do that by going against custom and marrying an Englishwoman, and in a church."

"That church is St. Paul's?"

"You got it. The article did not give a date when the wedding would be held. I asked Friar Xavier to look at the Queen's social calendar. He should be here soon."

♣♣♣

Everyone is talking at once. Michelle had arrived with Friar Xavier, not knowingly; he'd hitched a cab ride with her. He is in the process of explaining to me how he enjoyed traveling the city in a cab as compared to 'shanks mare'.

I introduce Michelle to Peter. She is telling him how miraculous it is that the wonderful, handsome, Inspector Boyle, had uncovered evidence in the rubble at the old kennel site, which led the police to the culprits. The suspected culprits and their homes are under observation. Since the evidence against Michelle was so thin, her solicitor was able to convince the authorities to let her go home but she cannot leave London.

Mick and Que-tip are arguing about the tracks and I'm getting a major headache. Why did I ever believe it was a gift to hear the Fae folk and spirits? I have to get rid of Michelle but how?

"I'm so glad that you're no longer under arrest. I just knew they were wrong. You could never have taken the dogs. I think the Queen will want to apologize to you personally, as soon as the dogs are found."

Everyone stops talking and stares at me as if I'm crazy. I silently tell them, *"Trust me guys, it is way too complicated to bring Michelle into this whole St. Paul's thing."*

"You know the best way to enjoy your new found freedom?"

"Pardon?"

"A shopping trip!"

Michelle actually squeaks and jumps up from where she is sitting with Peter. *"Oui,* I have seen the perfect dress…"

I stand up to move towards her and yelp, "Ouch, this darn ankle."

I'll never win an academy award for my acting, but Peter is so guilt ridden for bringing me into the tunnel that he doesn't notice.

"You are hurt. I forgot. No, no, how bad of me, I cannot go shopping. I will not think of leaving you. I must stay with you and be your Florence."

"My who?"

"The famous Englishwoman, she started the whole nursing thing. Without her women would probably not even be doctors today."

"Now I remember learning about her in school. She was named Florence because she was born in Florence, Italy. I love reading biographies of famous women, Florence Nightingale was my favorite." *Was she the spirit I met on the train, I wonder, why would she appear to me?*

"Please don't think you need to stay. You would be *so* bored. I'm going back to bed to rest. You do need to be prepared, think of all of those cameras and dignitaries. You *must* look your best. I have it, Peter will take you. I've my rental and he can drive you to the shops. It would be a favor to me *since we*, I mean *I can't do anything* today anyway." I look at Peter and hope he will understand and leave with Michelle.

"Are you certain Bridget?"

"Yes, Peter. I will be just great. Mick is here and he will see that I don't get into any trouble."

After a lot more fussing, getting ice and making me more tea, I was finally able to get them both to leave.

"Okay Friar, do you have the social calendar of the Queen?"

Friar Xavier looks at the nightstand by the bed and in a few seconds a flash of brilliant light appears, leaving behind an old fashioned, leather bound, hand written journal.

"Friar you didn't take the real one, did you?"

"No my dear, that is just a copy."

"Wow that sure beats Xerox."

I jump up off the bed and am pushed back down by three very determined entities. "Hey guys, relax, I'm fine. I was just trying to get rid of Michelle and Peter. He needs to cool it. He is so nervous I can't think."

I ran my finger down the list of entries and found one entitled *Lady Margaret Chaternning's wedding, S.P.C. at 10 A.M.*

"Well guys, it looks like we only have five days before the wedding. If I were the terrorists, I would not lay the bomb too early for fear it would be detected. They also cannot wait until the last minute. I think we need to go back down there today."

"Bridget, are you really up to another long walk?"

"Don't worry Mick; I will call a cab to take us right to the entrance of the old tube station. We know the way in, it won't be so hard. Hey, this is a piece of cake!" I burst out laughing at the puzzled looks on all three faces. I love using old expressions, their interpretations were priceless.

I dress in my 'cat burglar' outfit and gather my tools and two flashlights. I had called the cab company and was all set to leave when they showed up.

The street is crowded but walking a dog is always a good excuse to turn into an alley. The way is clear and soon we are inside the old station.

I remember to hug the wall. Friar and Que-tip had gone on ahead to make sure that we are alone. Mick stays close and I am smart enough to wear leather gloves this time and can hold onto the wall with no bad vibes. Just as I am about to jump down onto the tracks I have an overwhelming sense of fear. What the heck am I thinking? I heard stories of what they call the third rail, it's electrified. Heck, people die by touching it. Then there was the idea that I would be trapped down there and a train would come. I'm no Super Woman, no way. I'm going home.

"Bridget, please calm down. Take a deep breath. You cannot let your fears guide your life. If you ever want to achieve anything in this life you must let go of your fears."

"There you go again listening in on my thoughts. I thought we talked about this. My thoughts are off limit. Get it? Of course I'm worried about dying. You don't have that worry. You have what, nine lives?"

"That is said about cats, in case you have not noticed, I am a dog."

"Okay, let's get going. You know, you are wrong about fear, sometimes a good sense of fear keeps you alive."

I jump down onto the tracks and pray the twinge in my ankle will stop soon. I have way too much to do to let pain get in my way.

My heavy duty flashlight lit up the tunnel really well and I notice the 'third rail' and keep far away from it, just in case. We walk for what feels like ten city blocks, when we see a very bright light coming our way. I run back to where I notice a cut out in the wall that may have at one time held maintenance equipment. Just before I enter it, I hear, "Bridget we found something interesting."

I turn back; Friar and Que-tip were lit up like two bright searchlights. "Wow, turn those down a little guys, I can't see you."

"Sorry, little Miss Que-tip has some amazing talents."

"Why didn't you mention that the other day?"

"I did not want to let the creeps know we were down here and my light may have been noticed. This time I check out the tunnel, it is clear, so I turn on my high beams."

"Good job."

"What did you find?"

"Just ahead a bit, the tunnel bears to the right. Friar checked it out and the track on the right goes under the Cathedral. Further along the left track you come to the Exchange."

"The Exchange, that is like our 'Wall Street', like in stock exchange?"

"Right on."

"Is there any sign that anyone has been down here?"

"Nothing we can spot. Some very old traces of people, litter, graffiti, and things like that, nothing recent."

We all walk down to where the tunnel split. Only one track went to the right and one to the left. I wonder how they managed the schedule of train service back then. Well, I guess, not as many people meant that they did not need as many trains.

"If Mick can't smell recent traces of people, then we still may have time. If they haven't been down here yet, then they don't know of the split. Que-tip, one of the military guys the other night told us a story of a British stage magician; he was a famous magician or what they called an Illusionist who they used during the war to trick the Germans. I think we can do the same thing. George mentioned a new type of camouflage that the military uses. If we can get it, we can hang it from the ceiling and completely cover the opening that leads under the Cathedral."

"Minor problem, they will see the tracks leading that way."

"Not if we remove them."

"Que-tip, you once told me that some of your mates have special gifts. Can any of them lift heavy weights? Do you think that they can remove the track that goes to the right?"

"They may need some help. Their gifts are more to empower others with strength when they need it the most. You ever hear of a frail, ninety pound mother, lifting a car that was about to come down on her child? Well that is one of us giving her the power when she needs it most. That is the type of thing that we do."

"I know just the frail, ninety pound folks they can work with. Let's walk to the area under the Exchange; there is something I need to check out."

We walk the track until we are under the Exchange. We then went back to the place where the track split and walk until we are under the Cathedral, about the same distance.

"This may work. It is crazy guys, but it just may work."

When we get home a very tired and worried cousin is waiting for me.

"Peter, don't look so worried, it'll work. Remember the other night at the British Legion, George told us the story of Jasper Maskelyne, the British stage magician in the 1930s and 1940s."

"Yes, his 'Magic Gang' built a number of tricks. They used painted canvas and plywood to make jeeps look like tanks — with fake tank tracks — and tanks look like trucks. They created illusions of armies and battleships. But Bridget, make an entire tunnel disappear? We don't have Jasper around anymore."

"Jasper's largest trick was to conceal Alexandria and the Suez Canal to misdirect German bombers. He built a mockup of the night-lights of Alexandria in a bay three miles away with fake buildings, lighthouse, and anti-aircraft batteries. To mask the Suez Canal he built a revolving cone of mirrors that created a wheel of spinning light nine miles wide, meant to dazzle and disorient enemy pilots so that their bombs would fall off-target. Heck, all we have to worry about is a tunnel."

"Piece of Pie!"

"That's a piece of cake," I laughed, "but Que-tip is right, *we can do this.* All you need to do is to convince the veterans and I will go and speak with the faeire."

"How..."

"We don't have much time. They will try to set the bombs soon. I will also need to let my friend Charlie in on this. Hopefully he won't have me put into the loony bin and throw away the key."

Chapter 12

Stonehenge

Friar went with Peter. Que-tip went to round up the Fae. Mick and I head to the Fae meeting place at Stonehenge. We take the ramp onto Knightsbridge A4 and soon merge onto the M3. I feel proud that I am not only finding my way around England but also driving on the left side of the road. I did really well but Mick still groaned and hid his head beneath his paws at every roundabout. There has to be a bloody roundabout every mile or so.

"It's getting dark. I hope we get there soon."

We finally spot the sign for the Junction Eight exit towards Salisbury. Que-tip materialized on the dashboard just as I am pulling out of another roundabout. I jam on the brakes and pull to the side of the road.

Mike growls. *"Next time, ear wax, give a person a warning or something."*

I take a deep breath to calm my nerves, "Were you able to reach the others?"

"Sure, they are all waiting for you. Stay on this road and I will show you a back way in to avoid the tourists."

"But its dark already, won't they be gone?"

"You must be kidding mate. Night-time is when things heat up around here. There are always those who want to dance naked among the stones and the local constable has his hands full."

By the time I stop the car its pitch black. Funny how truly dark the country is without any lights from buildings or street lights. I turn off the car and step out onto a rocky, grass field. I stand for a moment to let my eyes adjust to the dark.

The night feels perfect. I can smell flowers of some kind and there is a mild breeze that brings warm air and a hint of music. Someone is playing a flute that sounds magical. The peaceful sound sweeps around me and takes away all the doubts and fears I have of meeting a roomful of Fae at one time.

I feel that I'm wrapped in a cocoon of peace. I look up at the sky and just then a meteor streaks across the sky, leaving a trail of glittering light behind. Wow, what a rush. I feel incredible, I wonder what's happening? Am I feeling the magic of Stonehenge?

Que-tip lit up to a soft glow and points the way. We walk for several minutes and stand beside a rock wall.

"Better size down for the entrance you two."

"Size down?"

"Don't tell me you have not mastered that yet."

Que-tip is looking at Mick accusingly.

"*I am getting to it. We must learn the basics first. Perhaps you could help us this time.*"

With a quick nod from Que-tip, I'm spinning. Soon I'm passing thru a long, narrow, tunnel of lights. I land as I had in Ireland on all fours. There has to be a better way of getting into these places. I feel dizzy but open my eyes to look around.

I have entered some kind of open-air fair with hundreds of Fae gathered around. There are folks walking around playing all sorts of instruments. Many of the ladies have flowers in their hair and a lot of the guys wear Robin Hood type hats with feathers. Everything is rainbow-hued with vivid sparkling colors and bright, multicolored flashes as more faeire arrive with their sparkling wings spread.

"I was thinking of maybe a dozen Fae, not hundreds."

"They all gathered here to meet you and bring back word of you to their tribes."

"There are more?"

"Our numbers are strong. There are as many Fae as there are humans, which is why we must not let Morrigan take control over all of us. She could cause great damage to the future of humankind if she is left to continue."

A faeire approached and bows before me.

"What the..., please don't do that. I'm just here to meet you. I'm your guest."

"As the prophecy predicted, you have come to us in our hour of need. My name is Emanon, I am the voice for us until I am taken over by Morrigan. Since that will be soon, I would like you to meet my second in command, David."

As Emanon nods, a young man flies from the crowd and kneels before me.

"Hey guys, please cut that out. It's making me feel weird."

Emanon nods and David stands. He's a little taller than me in this short form and so cute. Like Que-tip, his ears are pointed and his sky-blue eyes tilt just a little bit. The most noticeable difference between him and Emanon is his elfin face; it has mischief written all over it.

David bends his knee and removes a pointed hat with a very long feather, and sweeps it to his side. "Welcome, My Lady."

I couldn't help it, I laugh. "Sorry guys, but you look like you just stepped out of casting for a Three Musketeers movie. You also don't need to bow before me, I'm not royalty."

I hear a loud gasp and everyone starts speaking at once. Mick comes over and stands next to me.

"Attention Fae!"

Mick isn't speaking very loud but everyone is silent again.

"Bridget does not consider herself royalty. Although as we all know, she is of royal descent and actually is royalty. In her country, the United States of America, all people are equal. Hence her discomfort with being recognized as, how shall we say, special."

I hear a noise like leaves rustling in the trees, feel a strong breeze and look around. What an incredible sight, the Fae are clapping their wings. I had seen a few of the Fae land with wings outspread. As soon as they touch land they absorb their wings back into their bodies, as I've often seen Que-tip do. Now with all the wings on view, the room took on the look of a pirates' treasure chest, flowing over with precious jewels.

I move further into the room that resembles a crystal cave. "I'm very happy to meet all of you. My name is Bridget. I have recently heard of the troubles you are having. I promise I will do everything I possibly can to help. In my country there was a very wise leader by the name of Thomas Jefferson. He once said that 'When injustice becomes law, resistance becomes duty.' There can be no change until we all work together.

"Unfortunately I'm still in school." I hear a sigh, not one, but echoed a hundred times. The sound was so sad I could not hold back the tears. "What I mean is that my friend Mick here is still teaching me what I need to know to get Queen Geraldine back the throne her cousin took from her. I promise to learn as quickly as I can and get back to you with a plan, as soon as I have it."

They all applaud again and I find myself tear up. Wish they were tears of happiness but looking at the hopeful faces around me, I am struck with some major fears and doubts. How on earth am I to help them? I force myself to listen to the happy music and look at the beautiful spectacle in front of me and as Mick would say *'live in the moment'.*

The Fae celebrate. Many play instruments as they float in the air or dance among the others. I recognize most of them, there are guitars, fiddles, and ukulele, harp, drums, and another that resembles a smaller version of a cello.

I watch entranced by the sights and sounds. Soon I can feel the music under my skin and I also begin to laugh and dance. I feel great. I twirl around and move to the beat of old Celtic music. I feel so carefree, I can't stop laughing.

I feel someone staring and look down to see Mick. Who says that animals don't smile? I can see the curves of his mouth tilt up and many of his teeth are showing. His normally golden eyes have taken on the color of warm honey. I wonder what he's thinking.

"My lady?"

"Me?"

"Yes, my lady. Please follow me, the council is ready to commence."

We enter a large alcove. I hear a swishing sound and a clear, transparent film closes behind us. This cover completely stops all sounds from the party a few feet away. I look at the now serious faces forming a circle.

David begins the introductions. "As Emanon mentioned, in your language, I am called David. I coordinate the various council members and their activities. This is Deirdre, she and Alan are second in command."

I look at the dark haired couple. Both are smiling and obviously a couple. No wonder they share the position.

"This is Sam." A very handsome sandy haired man bows. "I work with your warriors, my lady. This is Cade, he is our strategist." A young guy with light brown hair, sparkling eyes and a beautiful smile comes over and bows.

The introductions continue. Half of their job duties I can't remember and many of the names I can't pronounce. Then David turns to a group of girls so different from one another but all with the same confidence and strength I have become used to with Que-tip.

Before he could continue with introductions, Que-tip spoke up, "Bridget, these are my mates; Brandie,

Brittney, Regan, Kearin, Samantha, Lindsey, Leonda, Tracey, Ana and Kasondra. We are in communications."

Deirdre looked puzzled, "RaeAnne, we are, all of us, in communications."

Aha, now I know Que-tips real name.

"I should have said that we are experts in communications. We encourage others to get the job done and done right." They all giggle.

David spoke up, "We hear that you are in need of illusionists, these men are the ones for the job." I look over at three young guys who resemble each other. "This is John, Joseph, and Thomas."

"Are they really illusionists?"

"No, but they are not afraid of hard work and will do whatever needs to be done to help you create an illusion."

"Thank you all for meeting with me. I need all of your help. As Mick mentioned, I'm still learning. There are so many skills that mortals are born with, that we don't know we have, because we seldom use them. I'm being confronted with challenges that I would not normally face, for the opportunity to realize what gifts I've been given. And to gain the confidence to reach for other gifts that may be available. The more I use my gifts, the more confidence I gain. With that confidence, will come the strength to help us defeat Morrigan. What I am facing now is a mortal challenge. Not only is a major spiritual symbol being threatened but we may also be facing a threat to the life of the Queen and all of the Royal Family..."

I speak with the Fae for several hours. Exhaustion is setting in. I feel Mick nudge my leg with his cold nose.

"You're right Mick. I've got to get home. Que-tip, could you fill them in on anything I missed. Goodnight everyone. Thank you again for your help."

A couple of girls appear and show Mick and me the way out. We find ourselves back under that magnificent ceiling of stars and back to normal size.

"Thank you, Kasondra and Ana. I don't feel as tired now; guess the cold air woke me up."

I stumble a few times but with the light provided by the faeire we find the car.

"Thanks again, please say goodnight to Emanon, I didn't see him at the meeting, was he busy?"

"Emanon left us at midnight; he is now beyond the age of reason."

I watch them fly off and still feel the sadness they left behind with those few words.

"Mick, we have to do something to help them. Morrigan can't continue her control of the Fae."

"We will do our best to stop her. I pray that it will be much later when we are more prepared. The Fae we met with are young. We can only hope that Cade is up to the strategy that will be needed to do battle."

"I really liked him. He is cute and smart. I think he will live up to any challenge he is given."

Chapter 13

The Plan

"What time is it Mick?"

"Straight up ten."

"Ten! Mick, why on earth did you let me sleep so long? We have a lot to do today!"

"You need your rest. Have a cup of tea and you won't be so grumpy."

"Peter should be here by now, where is he?"

"He will be here soon."

I jump up and run into the bathroom. "Thank goodness, my ankle is back to normal. I have so much to do today. I have to meet with Peter and the Vets from the legion. I have to remember to tell Peter that many of the Fae will meet us in the tube station so he won't be surprised. They will be able to help lift objects that our guys would not be able to on their own. I hope that the old timers were able to recruit some young guys to help also."

When the doorbell rang, I answer it while towel drying my hair, and open the door to find Peter standing there with six guys in their late twenties. The hunks have elite military stamped all over them from the way they are standing, and the haircuts. Behind them is a large black Humvee.

"Yikes, come on in, I will be back in a moment."

Great, I finally meet some cute guys and I look like a cartoon character with my 'fuzzy bunny' slippers and old fuzzy housecoat. I look up at Que-tip on top of the wardrobe.

"Cut that out, I can hear you giggle. It's not funny, how can I boss those guys around after they have seen me like this?"

"Ah, get over yourself. They will listen to you because you are smart and know what you are talking about. Not how you look. Go out there like the one in charge and you will be."

I quickly put on my old jeans, sweatshirt and sneakers. The front parlor is small but I never realized how small until it is filled with seven guys and a dog. They stop talking when I walk in and are staring at my chest. Okay, I know I have a good size chest but it has never stopped a room full of men talking. I am about to run back to the bedroom when I hear Mick laugh.

"Bridget me darling, what does that say on your shirt?"

I look down to see what top I have put on in my rush and laugh.

"Hi guys, this is a word we say a lot back home 'Forgetaboutit."

They all laugh. Peter comes over, puts his arm over my shoulder and introduces me.

"These guys are just back from the Stan, enjoying some R&R in London."

I whisper to Peter, "How much have you told them? Do they think we are crazy?"

"No, luv, no worry, worked on a case with Fred here a while back. He knows that when I say something will happen, it usually does."

"I can vouch for him, Miss. My mates and I have just the thing to get the job done."

"Great, you found some net?"

"Better than ordinary net, we have some Vizzy-Cloth, think you yanks call it Camo-cloak. Good stuff. It reflects the light, causing an optical illusion. The blokes will think they are looking at another tunnel wall. We will turn them around, that's for certain."

"That's so cool. Okay guys, let's get started. *Mick and Que-tip, once we get there, please go on ahead of us and make sure that we don't meet up with anyone."*

"Fred, you and Bridget take my car. I will hop in the Humvee with the guys and show them the way."

Peter is on a roll now. He no longer looks tired. He is doing something he loves, helping people in trouble. I'm enjoying myself also. I know that this is dangerous, but heck, I'm living life not just watching it on TV.

Peter leads the guys into the tunnel and explains our plan. I wait at the entrance for the vets from the legion hall. When they arrive I'm very surprised to see George has Maggie with them. They are out of breath. I should have driven over to get them, hope they didn't walk all the way.

"Okay girlie this is all of us that could make it. Did the guys from The Duke of Lancaster's 1st Battalion meet up with Pete?"

"Yes, they are in the tunnel now. Let's go inside so we don't attract too much attention and I'll let you know the plan."

One guy with an unlit pipe kept shaking his head. "Do you have a question Lloyd?"

"Why don't you call in the yard for this? We are old, we can't be any help."

"You have already helped. We have the guys below and they will hang a curtain to block off the entrance to the tunnel that goes under St. Paul's. Once we have the track removed that leads to that tunnel, no one will ever know it was there. That is when I will contact a friend at the yard and let him know that I think the Exchange is in danger. Hopefully the yard will set up surveillance and catch the guys in the act."

"Why can't they do that under St. Paul's?"

"I thought of that but I may not be believed and I don't want to take the chance."

It looks as if Lloyd is going to argue some more but just then Maggie starts laughing. It's so unexpected we all join in.

"The Yank has it right. They may think she's bonkers and ignore her over the church but do you think they will take a chance if someone threatens to mess with the country's money?"

I'd brought a small step ladder so no one had to jump onto the track. Peter's crew had also brought crow bars, torches to cut the track into smaller movable pieces, and wooden boxes the vets could sit on.

I nod to the Fae, each of the vets had company on their shoulders but the Fae were able to cloak so as not to be seen. Que-tip had explained to me that this ability comes close to the 'age of reason'. Before that it can be done but it takes a great deal of energy.

The Fae are to 'suggest' to the vets the best place to cut the track, and then assist them. Peter's crew would also help lift the track beyond the curtain. The vets would then take turns sweeping away any remaining traces of track left behind.

I stay by Lloyd and help him cut his first section of track. After the guys move his section we take a break and sit on the platform.

"I haven't done that much work in a long time. Didn't know I had it in me. I worked in the shipyards most of my life, welding mostly. I have always been fascinated by trains. Did you know that the Metropolitan Line was the first underground railway system in the world? It was built in 1863."

"I thought people were still in the horse and buggy stage around then. Some of the cities on the west coast of our country were not even settled by 1863."

I walk around to check on our progress. Two guys are up at the ceiling hammering in metal stakes to hold the curtain in place. Que-tip and her mates are keeping an eye on any possible opening where unexpected guests might catch us in action. Peter is busy with two guys further along the tunnel to St. Paul's.

"How's it going Peter?"

"The guys did not find anything. They have a device that will inform us if any charges have been laid. It is clean. Mick has not found any traces of humans since our last visit. Bridget, what if I am all wrong. What if it is not in a tunnel?"

"When this is done, why not ask the guys to make a sweep of the church, better safe than sorry."

"Good idea."

I hold my flashlight in front of me to watch where I'm walking and go deeper into the tunnel. I feel on edge again. What's wrong with me, besides the fact that I think I will be shot by a terrorist or killed by Morrigan? I feel it again, that feeling of being watched. I swing my light to the left and just see a black soot covered rock wall. I swing my light to the right and feel the hair on the back of my neck stand up. The light illuminates the black soot wall but it is blacker in one area and that area has the shape of a small person.

I do the only smart thing I can think of, I run as fast as possible back to people. I do the 'trip over your own feet' thing and land with a crash. I feel it before I see it, a blast of fire. I can feel the heat on my face. I bury my face in my hands and cry out, "Mick, I need you, Help!"

Mick and Que-tip materialize next to me.

"Stay down!"

Que-tip flies to my back and takes out her bow and arrow. If I wasn't so scared, I'd laugh. I've seen toothpicks bigger than that arrow. Mick sniffs the wall where the dark shadow was and then the wall that the flame hit.

"I'm surprised no one else is here, I would imagine panic would set in with a flame that size."

"I was able to sprinkle them all with a time spell. They will not see it."

"A time spell, hey that's real cool."

"Bridget, you really must study more magic. What is also cool is what I can do with this little toothpick, want me to show you?"

"Oops, sorry about that, it's just laughter taking the place of the hysterics I don't have time for."

"Whoever it was did not leave a trail. I know one thing, this villain is not human. Morrigan knows you are not dead."

"Great, but why doesn't she come after me herself."

"It is her way to show that you are insignificant, anyone can kill you, that assassin was probably her least experienced."

"Thanks a lot. If I didn't trip, he would have succeeded. That flame would have hit me directly. Good thing I'm clumsy. I was so scared I even forgot to set the protective shield in place."

Que-tip and Mick exchange a look.

"So out with it, what's with the look?"

"Bridget there are no accidents. Often what we cry over is just something minor that has happened to prevent something major happening."

"Like I have a bruised body instead of being a fried crispy critter?"

"*Exactly! Bridget even though you may not have remembered to protect yourself, your instincts kicked in and raised the shield. The heat you felt was the flame striking the shield. Que-tip and I can see the marks of flame all around you.*"

"That thing hit me?" I shake off the fear the only way I know, "Okay guys, enough rest, time to get back to work. Do you think we can finish this today?"

"We will finish. You and Mick are to return home."

"But Que-tip, I need...?"

"We are close to our goal. Do you think the Fae want you in harm's way?"

"Okay, but make sure you have the vets rest every fifteen minutes or so. I know you guys are doing all the work but I don't want anything happening to them."

"It will be done. Now go home and work with Mick to strategize how you will defeat Morrigan."

"Yeah, I hear ya. Nothing too difficult, just stop the 'Goddess of War', yeah, yeah, yeah, easy for you to say."

I know they're right. I've been keeping busy with this to avoid dealing with the bigger picture. Someone wants to kill me. I have had too many 'accidents' happen lately, the chair at the Spa, the guy in the tube station. Maybe my assailant was influenced by one of Morrigan's followers and then had a change of mind. I don't know. That is the big problem, I don't know what to expect. I don't know what is coming next or who it may be. Anyone who is not strong in their own beliefs can be influenced by evil.

Chapter 14

Back to Bed

He's close. He's carrying a light in his left hand and in its glow I can see him. He is tall and familiar. I can see the sleeve of his jacket. It is red and shiny, like satin. It has embroidery in gold, very exotic. He's...

"Bridget, wake up."

I wake up to Mick licking my face. "Darn it Mick, I almost saw him this time. I know him, at least I have seen him before, but who is he?"

"Who?"

"The guy who's going to blow up the church, that's who."

"I think it is time you tell me again of this vision."

"You're right." I tell Mick what happened when I fell on the stairs at the station. I leave off the part where I'm shot. He and Que-tip will pack me away to a deserted island, and I have to finish this.

"I'm having all kinds of nightmares and encounters with evil Fae...."

"What other...?"

"Bridget, I hope I am not interrupting."

I watch as Friar Xavier materializes next to my bed. I feel Mick growl and realize I have my arm around him. Holding onto him for comfort has become a habit. Holding or petting an animal always makes me feel good, but holding Mick makes me feel something special, like safe.

"That's okay Friar, we were just talking about my nightmare. How are things at the Palace?"

"That is why I am here."

There was a quick flash on the bed next to me and my nerves must be worse than I thought. I squeeze Mick too hard and he yelps, *"Take care, it is only the good Friar, and his magic."*

"Sorry Mick."

I pick up the fancy envelope. "What's this Friar?"

"You may wish to attend the reception for the wedding party. If one has an invitation it is much easier to enter. The Hotel will be heavily guarded."

I open a heavy vellum envelope lined with gold foil. The invitation is embossed with a royal crest and the lettering is also in gold.

"OMG, it'll be held at the Savoy on the Strand. I could see it from the London's Eye, it's beautiful. I would love to go, but I can't."

"You are finally getting some common sense."

"What do you mean Mick?"

"Sorry Friar, Bridget had an encounter today with one of Morrigan's henchman. She is too frightened to go."

"I am *not* too frightened to go anywhere. I just don't belong there. I will never fit in and what on earth would I wear?" I could tell that Mick and Friar Xavier were smiling but I refuse to look at them.

"Well, I guess it would be good to see the wedding party up close. I might be able to sense who the villains are. Maybe I could get an outfit that doesn't cost too much. There is that resale shop in the East End that I want to check out. What do you think Mick?"

"You should be safe there. Perhaps your gift will allow you to determine who the villains are and we could watch to see when they enter the tunnel."

I look at the date on the invite.

"Yikes, I only have a few days. I have to call Michelle, time to go shopping."

"Why call Michelle?"

"An important outfit like this calls for girl time."

"Did I hear you say shopping?"

"Hi Que-tip, how are things in the tunnel?"

"The tracks are moved to the right hand tunnel. You cannot see where they were. The curtain is completely covering the tunnel entrance to St. Paul's. You would have to get close and actually feel the wall to realize it is not soot covered rock. It looks great. Enough of dark, dirty tunnels, I want to go shopping."

"Of course you can come. I'll call Michelle."

Chapter 15

Shopping

I quickly change and just have time to grab my Coach handbag with Que-tip safely hidden away inside when Michelle arrives.

"Don't worry Mick. Morrigan won't know that I'm still alive. It will take her awhile to find out and get another assassin lined up. Go play outside, Que-tip will keep an eye on me."

I run out the door almost knocking down Michelle before Mick continues demanding that he come along.

Michelle has her small Fiat parked out front and we laughingly run through the morning drizzle.

"Where do you wish to go first, Bridgette?"

"I hear that there are some great vintage pieces at The East End Thrift Store. Let's try that first."

"Okay but I insist that if you do not find what you want there, that next we go to Kings Road in swinging Chelsea. The shops there are my favorite and I have to show you where I found my outfit to meet the Queen."

I luck out at The East End and we found just the perfect formal wedding reception outfit. Michelle picked it out. It is a pretty floral prom dress for what she calls that *quintessentially English look.*

It does have that traditional English rose look. Never thought I would be wearing flowers but the strapless prom dress look, with a netting underskirt and sash tie is to die for. I even found a hat and matching shoes.

What a kick, I can't wait to show Mary. I wonder where Simon and Mary are now. What would they say about this latest adventure? Sure wish I could call them. It's frustrating not having anyone to talk to about the ghosts and Fae. Mary would understand. Michelle is okay to talk clothes with. She likes fashion a whole lot better than Mary does. Guess it is good to have a variety of friends. Oh well, Mary will be home soon, I hope.

Michelle looks at me a little funny when I purchase the little flower girl crown, with tiny flowers and a long veil.

"Just a little something, I think a friend of mine will like."

Que-tip is sound asleep in my purse after wearing herself out, flying from one display to another. Thank goodness she was able to keep herself somewhat invisible. She wouldn't have stopped until I told her I would buy the flower girl crown and warned her about seeing the shopkeeper grab a fly swatter.

We had fun shopping and a great lunch.

Michelle drops us off at the door and I let myself in.

"Mick, are you home?"

I look outside but he's gone. I pick up a sleeping Que-tip and place her on my pillow and quietly close the door. I let out a long sigh and decide I need Mary.

"Hi Mary, how are you?"

The cell is a little scratchy but I can still hear her, she sounds happy.

"Hi Bridge, we are doing great. You would not believe all of the great places we have seen. I have kept notes so that you can go see them for yourself someday. How are things going?"

"That is why I called, I have been busy sightseeing and..."

"Oops sorry Bridge got to go. We're entering a tunnel and I will lose you. Can you believe it, we are driving to France. Bye, I'll call again soon, promise."

I stare at my cell phone for a minute, sit back in the old armchair, cover myself with a blanket, and cry over the end of the way things used to be. I guess the closeness Mary and I shared for over ten years is still there, just a little different.

We're still like sisters. We have too much history not to be. We went to the same school. I would be at her place more than mine. I think her Mom knew what life was like for me and dad. He was never home when he was sober. Then he stopped coming home.

When Mary found out that I'd been evicted, her Mom didn't hesitate to let me share their studio apartment with them. Although it was crowded with the three of us, it felt more like home than any place I ever lived. Guess I am on my own again. Just have to get used to it. I laid my head back...

The scraping noise is coming closer. He's carrying a light. He's wearing a fancy outfit. He smiles. My feet are frozen in place, I open my mouth to yell for Mick but no sound comes...

I hear a low growl. Shake myself awake and rub my eyes. My fingers come away wet.

"Sorry Mick, I must've fallen asleep. Did you have a good day?"

Chapter 16

The Reception

Thank goodness for the lavish flower arrangements, they're everywhere, in urns and baskets, on the tables, pedestals and even the floor. I slip behind a large arrangement to avoid the welcoming line. I keep talking to myself to calm my nerves. *My outfit looks okay, I can blend in. Just breathe.*

I look at the crowd gathered in the most beautiful room I've ever seen. These are folks from the who's who of royalty. I feel I'm in a magazine. I see Princes Victoria of Sweden, Queen Rania of Jordan, the Duchess of Wessex and many more whose names I can't remember. I can feel my heart race, turn and head back to the door.

What on earth am I thinking? They'll find out that I'm a party crasher and lock me up. I don't belong here. Not only are these guys way out of my league but they're royalty for goodness sake.

I'm almost back to the entrance when I hear Mary's mom, *"Get back in there young lady. Do you think you are so high and mighty that you cannot sit with other folks? They'll stop what they're doing to just look at you?"* I stop walking and start laughing, just as I did when she said those words to me ten years ago.

Once a month Mary and her mom would dress up in their Sunday best and have a cup of tea at some swank hotel or restaurant in Manhattan. The first time they brought me with them I was sick to my stomach and ran out. Mary's mom knew I felt that I was not good enough to sweep the floor in a fancy place, no mind sit down and drink tea. As far back as I could remember I had to beg for food or beg landlords not to evict us. I'd often been called *'Street Trash'* and believed it.

Just as she did back then, she put her arm through mine, told me to put my head up, shoulders back and said, 'Remember young lady, God created you, He created me and all them folks in this place. God makes no trash.'

I dash into the restroom and touch up my makeup. I really miss Mary and her Mom. I feel they're with me. I'll make them proud and help Peter do this. I leave the safety of the restroom and boldly walk over to the buffet line, fill my plate with a little of everything: lobster, pate, curry chicken, prime rib. Wow what a spread. No shortage of money in this crowd. There is no way I can eat all this, but it will give me an excuse not to talk to anyone.

I just finish the lobster when the people from the welcoming line take their seats. There are two dark skinned, middle-eastern looking men sitting on either side of Lady Margaret. The young prince is holding her hand, looking so proud and happy, smiling at everyone. Wow, what a catch, he's hot.

I notice two things at once. The guy I assume is his brother is not wearing glasses. He looks fierce and angry. He could be the older brother, he gives me the creeps. He doesn't look like the guy in the tunnel. Darn, I should have gone up to them in the welcoming line. I look at all the other middle-eastern guests and no glasses.

I wonder if it's a henchman in the tunnel, but the clothes were so exotic looking. Whoever it is must have money and be dressed up for the wedding. None of these guests feel like a mass murderer. I give up. I'm not the most confident sensitive in the world under the best of circumstances and right now I'm weary to the bone. I think I have lost faith in my *magical abilities.*

Right on cue, Friar Xavier materializes on the chair next to me. *"Any luck Bridget?"*

"Sorry Friar, wish I could pick him out of the crowd, but I can't. Maybe it's not precognition. Maybe my dream was just an ordinary, run of the mill nightmare."

"Perhaps in the moment you were only able to make out certain features. It is often that way at a moment of stress."

"You're right. I read that victims of crimes have a very hard time giving descriptions of their assailant for that very reason. So it isn't just me."

"Pardon?"

"Thank you Friar Xavier, you're the best. I was beginning to doubt my abilities and it's just my human side working against me. I will let go of my physical description and look only with my 'inner eye' to really see the people around me."

"Then I will leave you to it. Good luck dear Bridget, God is with you."

I push my dinner plate away and take a long drink of water. I walk into the lobby away from the music and noise and find a quiet corner with a beautiful marble fountain. The sounds of running water and the beautiful plants help to ground me and remove any doubt in my ability to get the job done. I take a few deep breaths and begin to gather my inner strength as Mick has taught me.

I walk back into the room and begin to check out people's auras. I narrow it down to one person at a time and it takes a long time. I can see bright colors showing the enjoyment of the day and some dark shades of grey. Noticing nothing out of the ordinary, I turn to focus on the wedding party again. I'm too late. They're no longer at their table.

I move quickly to catch up with them and catch sight of a wraith at the corner of my eye. What's that? It's not friendly. I can't see anyone. Not a friendly spirit or Fae. I have the feeling I'm being watched. I can't call Mick or Que-tip. I haven't seen anything solid or identifiable. Something is here with me.

I now know where the expression 'makes my skin crawl' comes from. Are the nightmares getting worse? Am I hallucinating? If it's a spirit I would see it, right?

I snap out of my daze just in time to bump into a waiter and fall in the midst of a large tray of plates he's carrying into the kitchen. Food is flying everywhere. I watch in shock as a large plate of goose pate hits a woman wearing an enormous hat shaped like an orchid. Red wine makes its way to a woman in a pure white sari. I jump up and bend to help pick up some of the plates but fall again as I bump heads with a gorgeous guy.

Oh Wow! Now this cutie, I'll never forget. He looks out of place at this stuffy reception. More like a model with shoulder length sun-bleached hair curling in waves to his shoulders, a deeply tanned distinctive face.

Mr. Hottie has his arm around me and is helping me out to the lobby. He's so strong I feel like I'm floating. Oh my, I turn to thank him and my mouth won't work. He is looking at me with the most beautiful golden eyes and those lashes are to die for, laugh lines frame his eyes ... What the...?

He's laughing at me! He's pointing at me and laughing. What a jerk, I pull away from him and march over to the elevator. I push the button to go down to the parking garage. The elevator doors open, and I get a look at myself in the full length mirror. Well it doesn't look like a fancy creation shaped like an orchid but wearing a lobster in my hair did look original. I start laughing and turn back to thank Mr. Hottie. He's gone, dang it.

Chapter 17

Meeting with Charlie

"Bridget, I think it's time for you to call in Scotland Yard."

"You're right Friar, but I don't know if they will believe me."

"I have never had them listen to me. I think I am on their records as a mental case, otherwise I would go in your place."

"Thank you Peter, but I know Charlie. I've helped him twice now and I think he'll listen to me. Hopefully he'll have enough pull to have the tunnels put under surveillance."

"We can only try, Bridget. You have other matters on your plate right now. It is time to turn this over to the local law enforcement."

"I hate to find myself agreeing with flea-bite but he is right. You must prepare for Morrigan. I can read something new in your aura Bridget. Have you another encounter with the flame thrower from the tunnel?" asked a puzzled Que-tip.

Everyone started talking at once.

"Calm down guys. I don't know what it is. Maybe it's stress causing the dark areas in my aura, Que-tip. Would dark spots show up if you are overly worried about something?"

"Added to the stress you are already under, I would say so."

Friar left his seat on my fireplace mantel and is now pacing the floor in step with Peter. Mick was sitting at my feet staring at me and Que-tip is perched on the arm of the couch. They are all waiting for me to explain.

"Okay guys, yesterday at the reception, just seconds before the waiter bumped into me, I thought I saw something. A wraith, a spirit, something flashed by so quickly I couldn't make out what it was. I wouldn't be upset except that I sensed an evil blackness like I've never felt before."

"Are you certain that the feeling was coming from the spirit and not from a person in the room?"

"Dang it Friar, I hadn't thought of that. Here I'm putting out feelers to read auras and I received a hit at the same instant that I caught the movement and I assumed that they both were connected. If the feeling of evil wasn't coming from whatever was watching me, then it must have come from a human source. The man I was after was there at the reception. I bet the older brother, Prince Oama, walked by me and I didn't notice. We can't take any chances this late in the game. Que-tip, do you think that you could assign a faeire to watch Prince Oama and report his movements back to us?"

"Certainly," she responds and is off.

"What about the younger Prince?"

"I'm hoping that he'll be so busy with wedding plans and keeping his beautiful fiancée amused, he won't have time for anything else. If I'm reading this right, he and his bride and the Queen will be safe until the wedding day."

"You are thinking that the older Prince will take out his own brother?"

"Well, from what I've read, the young prince is gaining a lot of followers in their country. He could overthrow his brother and gain control. What a perfect opportunity for Prince Oama. He can remove a potential threat to his throne and turn the followers that are in favor of 'western ways' against England."

"Bridget, how do you think of such things?"

"I love to read Mick. I never read until I moved in with Mary. They had books everywhere and I did a lot of reading. I got used to it and now cannot think about going to sleep unless I read a chapter or two. I read anything I can get my hands on. History is great. That is where you learn about governments being overthrown by siblings."

"Interesting."

"Someone told me that history keeps repeating itself. That everyone should learn history so that we can prevent the worst of it from happening again."

"What do you want me to do Bridget?"

"I hate to ask this of you Peter, but could you keep Michelle busy. They have not caught the dog-nappers yet and she's a nervous wreck. Take her to the coast or something. There's nothing any of us can do at this point. I'm going to see Charlie and ask him to add surveillance cameras in the tunnels."

"Okay Bridget, you are right, it is better to keep busy. Call me anytime; I will not be too far away."

"Thank you Peter, I'll call Charlie now and set up a meeting."

Interlude

The Dorgis

"Que-tip, I think the police are close to finding the criminals that took Queen Mum's dogs."

"Great news Lynne, are you still tagging along after that Inspector?"

"I don't let him out of my sight. I will let you know as soon as we have them in hand."

"Are you okay with leaving Willie on his own?"

"I have Kasondra and Natalie keeping an eye on him."

"Brilliant, keep at it."

Chapter 18

Help Wanted

I set the meeting for the little park across from Charlie's office.

"What are you thinking Bridget? There is no way I can get the blokes at the yard to go along with this. They will want to know who my informant is, run it up the chain of command and then it will go into committee. It will take weeks."

"We don't have weeks. My source tells me that this will take place within the next couple of days. What can we do?"

"Let me think on it. I will let you know. You do trust your source?"

"One hundred percent."

"I will get back to you."

"When Charlie? I must know if you will do something or not."

"If I say no, then what, you will set up surveillance yourself?"

"If I have to."

"Are there more at home like you?" he laughs, shakes his head and gets up to leave, bends over and pats Mick on the head, "nice dog."

"I'll 'nice dog' him."

"Mick, he's just being friendly, what's the matter?"

"It sounds as if you will get no help from that direction."

"You never know, Charlie may be able to do it."

I look at Mick and laugh. *"Okay, let's think of what to do. What's plan 'B', if Charlie cannot set up surveillance in the tunnel?"*

"You were hoping that Charlie would set up electronic surveillance that would be monitored by the professional, round the clock, 24 hour security staff of the Exchange. That is what is really needed. I have it, call Miss Ear-Wax."

"Call Que-tip, why... Oh, I know, good thinking. You really need to stop calling her ear wax, it really gets her mad."

"I know, that is why I do it."

I shake my head at Mick, *"Let's call her from the car so she can materialize without having to use energy to stay invisible."*

"Thanks for coming Que-tip. I'm not sure Charlie will be able to get the help we need on his own. He's a great guy but he doesn't have the clout to pull the strings we need to get this done in a hurry. Can you and the other 'communication' ladies get to work on all the members of the yard that Charlie reports to?"

"Piece of pie!"

In a whirlwind of sparkling dust, Que-tip goes off to work her magic. I let out a deep breath and lay my head back on the headrest.

"Mick, what else can I do? I helped Friar by finding a clue that helped to uncover the identity of the dog-nappers. I helped Peter to camouflage the tunnel entrance that leads under St. Paul's and set it up so the would-be terrorists would get caught attempting to blow up the Exchange. Did I miss anything?"

"I do not believe so. Why, do you feel that there is something left undone?"

"Maybe I just need to get some sleep. Maybe what is nagging at the back of my mind will come to me when I dream. Just hope I wake up and remember what the answer is."

"You do not look as if you got much sleep."

"Thanks, I look that bad huh? I can't seem to get the feeling out of my head that I'm missing something. Let's start with the dog-nappers. Why? What would a pair of third rate thieves hope to gain by stealing the Queen's dogs? They are not bright enough to plan it on their own. Someone must be familiar enough with Sandringham House to have known the layout.

"They must have wanted the attention of the world to be on the dog-napping. Why steal something that belongs to a wonderful lady who is loved by so many. What would you accomplish?"

"Do you know how many billions of people around the world love animals? If they do not have feeling for the Queen, just remember the headline's and pictures of cute puppies. Here you have a sweet old lady who loves animals, and someone is causing her pain by taking her loved ones away, and perhaps harming them. That news

caused a great deal of emotion. How did you feel when you read the news?"

"I felt anger and pain. I want to do something to those evil men."

"Then you are not the average reader. Oftentimes when one reads something that causes so much emotion, it takes us to an even more evil place within, the desire for revenge. Some folks want the evil doers to suffer. Sometimes they have a preconceived notion of who the evildoers are and retaliate in small ways. Forwarding negative emails or commenting negatively on the World Wide Web. In this case, the world is focused on France as the evil doer behind the dog-napping. What is happening in France that world opinion would hurt?"

"Wait, I read something before all of this started. France wants to be the next home of the summer Olympics. They were number one in the standing and the decision was to be made next week."

"That could be it then. If world opinion is against a country, the Olympic committee would never select them."

"We need to find out what country is now the number one choice to win the spot as the host of the next summer Olympics. Wait, I'll Google it."

"What did you find?"
"This is crazy, I can't believe it."
"What country?"

"Us! The United States of America is now at the top of the list. How could someone from my own country do something so low?"

"We are .... I mean people are human, and humans, no matter where they live can be influenced by evil, if they allow themselves to be."

"That is why I have to stop Morrigan from using the Fae to influence people. To encourage evil acts."

"It sounds like her work."

"I don't understand. It must be some big corporate owner who is not satisfied with only making a few billion, he wants to make more. Why are folks so greedy? And don't tell me television; I have heard that one before."

"You are correct, there is some proof that your television does make people feel that they need more things to be happy. That they are deprived if they do not have the latest must have *item. This is at a higher level. Your average corporate leader is obsessed with the bottom line, in making more money. They seldom stop long enough to appreciate the blessings they already have."*

"Charlie said that they are monitoring the bank accounts of the guys they believe took the dogs. They think one of them will come out of hiding long enough to pull the money from the bank account and they can pinpoint an area to search. I'll let him know our theory and see if he was able to follow the money trail back to the person that paid them to do this. Anything we can do to get France back in the running with the Olympic committee?"

"That is the power of negative thinking. It takes a great deal of good to overcome the smallest seed of ill feelings, whether against a person or a country."

"So when people hear that an American was behind this hideous crime, they will not just blame that one person. World opinion will be against all of us and not just the idiot that did it."

"I am afraid so, it is always the case. Remember your history."

"Sometimes talking to you is depressing. I'm going to call Charlie to fill him in and see if he has any news for us. Then I'm going to have a cup of tea and call Mary and talk about fun stuff."

Interlude

Surveillance

Lynne sits on the brim of Charlie's hat as he waits in a van parked on Oak Street.

"Cade, are they still inside?"

"Yes, they are arguing as usual. It is hard work getting these guys quiet enough to plant any suggestions."

"Charlie and his team are in place. Let me know when to nudge him along."

"Right On."

"Okay Lynne, David and I finally got through to them. They are leaving now for the pub."

Charlie is texting. Lynne flies down to his ear and whispers. "Look out the window now."

"Those are our guys. Brad, you, and Steve follow them. We will go inside and make sure the dogs are here before we make our arrest."

"Cade, how are the puppies?"

"Sleeping, but not natural like, I bet the bloody creeps used a drug to knock them out.

"I checked they are all alive."

"Thank you David, I will make sure that Charlie calls Bridget right off."

Chapter 19

The Pups Are Home

"Great news guys, that was Charlie on the phone, they got the guys who took the puppies. Best of all, the puppies are all okay. They found evidence that they had been put to sleep with ether but they recovered from that. The only problem now is that they have been given the run of the palace and the Queen is having so much fun playing with them that nothing else is getting done."

The small front room filled with sparklers as Que-tip twirled and Friar danced around with her. Peter is laughing at the strange sight. Mick comes over to me and nudges my arm with his nose. I automatically lift my arm to hug him.

"Good job my girl; you have made many, many people happy today."

I laugh and hug him tight. "Time to celebrate! How about tea and cookies or I may have some leftovers, we could make some sandwiches?"

"My treat Bridge, I will just pop over to the fish and chips stand and get us all a proper meal."

"Sounds great to me," I look around at my new family of friends and suggest, "Better get some extras, maybe a hamburger or two and a milkshake."

Que-tip twirls around some more and yells "Yippee," Oops, she twirls so fast she bumps into the television. I think I better watch her sugar intake.

♣♣♣

While we eat supper, we watch an old rerun of 'Upstairs, Downstairs', I look over at Que-tip, she is lying on Peter's shoulder and they are both asleep. The Friar is watching everything on TV, especially the commercials, they are his favorite. His latest game is trying to figure out what the advertiser is actually trying to sell. He very seldom figures it out, but when he does, he dances around for awhile and then settles down to watch some more. Mick is also asleep with his head on my lap. It feels good just to relax. I lay my head back against the couch...

I am back in the tunnel. *A scream echoes thru the tunnel, a cry that came from the heart of a nightmare. It reverberates for a long moment and then deadly silent. I now understand the true meaning of the word bloodcurdling. The blood ...*

"Bridget wake up, please wake up, it is only a dream."

I open my eyes. Mick is standing on my lap, nose to nose with me. His scratchy tongue is licking my face. I shake my head.

"I'm okay Mick it's only a dream."

I look into his beautiful eyes, so filled with concern *for me.* I feel a strange pull in the vicinity of my heart, like a vise gripping me hard. I love this little guy. I don't know how I ever survived without him.

"What is going on, are you okay Bridget?"

"I'm fine Peter, honest, I'm okay guys, it was just a scary dream."

"What was it about, it may be important."

"I don't think so, guys let's have a cup of tea and plan what we are going to do tomorrow. What time should we be at the Cathedral?"

"Half eight."

"Okay, I'll be there at eight-thirty, the service starts at ten. Will I have any problem getting into the main chapel that early?"

"I am not certain what security measures are in place. Have you heard from your friend at the yard?"

"Sorry guys, I was so excited about the puppies that I totally forgot the other great news. Charlie, with a lot of help from our Fae friends, was able to get some very high-tech surveillance equipment that will alert them to any entry under the Exchange."

"The buggers may be looking for such equipment and be prepared to dismantle it."

"You're right Peter, they thought of that. They want them to think that the tech alarm is the only one. They also installed trip wires."

"Trip wires?"

"It's an old fashioned set-up Que-tip, not something these guys will be expecting. Sometimes they are connected to a bomb that goes off when the wire is triggered. In this case the wires are connected to an alarm that sounds above ground in the security office. It's the best they can do for a back-up plan."

"Where do you want me?"

"Peter, we know that the Royals are also a target. The Queen and her family are well protected. I am not sure about the bride-to-be. If you could just stroll by the home of Lady Margaret and see if you sense anything off, you know what I mean?"

"Excellent, should I meet up with you in the American Chapel?"

"Yes, if you can, you may not be able to get through the crowd."

"I'll text you my whereabouts, be sure to keep your mobile on."

"I will, it takes getting used to, but I like having it handy."

"Friar, you of course will be next to the Queen. Quetip, could you and your team go in early and check the area for anything that does not feel right. The Queen's security will check for bombs as normal routine for any place she may be, but we may be wrong about the tunnel, or they may have changed their minds and will use another means."

"I will stay with you."

"Sorry Mick, you can't stay with me. I want to go into the Cathedral myself and you will not be allowed in."

"I will accompany you."

"You can wait just outside the door. I will be fine. If they are checking for bombs inside the Cathedral and we know that we have the tunnels covered, I will be fine. Don't worry so much. You'll get wrinkles and wind up looking like a Blood Hound."

Chapter 20

Wedding Day

I thought eight-thirty way too early to be up and about on a Saturday morning, but these folks didn't. At least a hundred people are walking about taking pictures or doing last minute tasks. I enter the main part of the cathedral which is situated under a high domed ceiling. I stand in awe, in a large open space that must be able to seat at least a thousand people. The floor of the cathedral is tiled in a black and white checkerboard pattern that is a brilliant backdrop for the red roses women are placing, in small bouquets, to the end of each aisle.

Everywhere I look there are flower arrangements. Large bundles of white carnations, lilies and roses. Added into all that white are deep, dark, red roses, which really stand out to make a dramatic statement. Wish they didn't remind me of blood spilled on a wedding gown. Yuck.

I pass a woman who looks like a wedding planner. She is dressed in a dark red silk dress with a matching red and white short jacket, standing with several guys in tuxes. Talk about color coordinating, even her clipboard is red.

I walk down the narrow hallway between the pillars looking, for what, I don't know. I wish my Sherlock sense would kick in soon. I know that something is not right but I have no idea what. Up ahead is the 'Great Circle' under the dome and, beyond that I can see the choir gathered for a final practice.

A few hundred steps above me, I can make out men in uniform making the rounds of the three circular galleries that make up the inside of the dome, their reports to each other echoing off the walls in scary sounding whispers. I duck behind one of the pillars when I spot one of the Queen's guards setting up gold rope barricades, and asking tourists to move on. He is explaining that this section is being closed off due to the upcoming wedding. Of course this just excites folks and they stay around taking pictures. Many look like they are ready to camp out and wait to see the Queen. Wonder how that will work for them.

I wander around, keeping out of sight of the guard. The choir begins singing a hymn. The wedding planner walks by with her entourage, "The bridal party will then move to the Ambulatory to sign the Registers." She stops, looks at me, decides I am not important to the wedding and continues on. *Well that felt weird.*

I give up, my spidery sensors are not working. I sit down in a pew and say a quick prayer for guidance. As I bend my head, I spot a colorful brochure lying on the floor. I pick it up and read the cover, "The Insiders Guide to St. Paul's."

"Within the cathedral are plaques, carvings, monuments and statues dedicated to a wide range of people. The bulk are related to the British military with several lists of servicemen who died in action - the most recent being the Gulf War. There are special monuments to Admiral Nelson and to the Duke of Wellington, on horseback, unveiled in 1912. Be sure to visit our famous Crypt.

"Entrances to the downstairs crypt are in both transepts, on either side of the dome. St. Paul's substantial cathedral crypt contains over 200 memorials as well as another chapel and the treasury. Many notable figures are buried in St. Paul's Cathedral crypt, such as Florence Nightingale and Lord Nelson.

"The treasury has very few treasures. Many were lost over the years. It is unknown how the thieves gained entry through the crypt. Some speculate that it was by means of a secret passage used in 1810 when a major robbery took almost all of the remaining precious artifacts, its location remains a mystery."

OH no! There can't be another way in that we don't know about. Maybe it's another entrance to the Underground tunnel. I run the length of the long hallway to the back of the main floor. At the east end of the Cathedral, behind the High Altar, is the American Memorial Chapel. To the right of that are stairs I noticed on my last visit here.

I continue to move quickly while trying not to draw the attention of the guards. I look again at the Choir and Altar and get a tightening in my chest of the history and beauty that may be destroyed if I don't stop this.

I finally reach the stairs and find a large red velvet cord blocking the entrance to the stone steps leading down to the lower floors. 'No Entrance without prior approval! Visitors must be accompanied by a church guide.'

"No way, Jose! No time!" I lift up my Dolce Cabana pencil skirt, exposing more skin than should be shown in these halls, and step over the rope. The stone steps are worn in the center and totally uneven. I almost take a header down the entire flight and grab the railing. I remove my shoes and continue down what must be equal to two long flights of steps. *"I really must remember to donate some money to this place; they seriously need more lights down here."*

I walk down the hallway to a vaulted room, labeled 'Nelson Chamber'. I look in and see a black sarcophagus, but no door. I continue down the hallway to another room. I see a simple casket made of granite with the name Arthur Wellington. *"Wow, I have to come back and check that out later. That's the Duke."*

After minutes that seem like hours of running around in circles, I stand under a dimly lit light bulb and check the brochure to see if I have missed something. Where is the Treasury?

"The crypt of St. Paul's is the largest in Western Europe, and unusual for a cathedral, is the exact 'footprint' of the cathedral floor."

No wonder I can't find this place. Okay think... the Choir was the first part of the cathedral to be built. If the Treasury of artifacts was here, it would be in the oldest part of the building. As with most churches, built during the same time of this one, it is shaped like a cross.

I retrace my steps to the center of the crypt and go from the west side of the building to the east side and then I find the less elaborate tombs and the room dedicated to the Treasury.

Of course it has a door and of course, it is locked. The old fashioned lock doesn't look as if it's been open in a long time, now what? A credit card won't work to open that. What if alarms go off if I open it? If it hasn't been opened, then no one else has gone in. Maybe the door is elsewhere?

I walk over to a light and check the brochure again. I read something, but what. I know I was given this for a reason, but what? Come on Bridget think, where is the other entrance to the tunnels?

"Bridget, it is half-nine, where are you?"

"Mick, I can't explain now but please go to the underground, directly beneath the Cathedral and see if you can find another opening?"

"Where are you?"

"I'm in the crypt under the choir area. The crypt is below street level about equal with the underground tunnel. I just read that there was a break-in here in 1810. I am looking for another opening to the tunnel. If there is one it may be set with explosives and our camouflage trick in the tunnel won't work. Please hurry!"

"I am not going anywhere without you. You must leave the Cathedral now! Peter has had no word from Charlie that the culprits have been captured, have you heard from him? The explosives may go off at any moment. Get out of there!"

"They will wait until the service is underway and all the guests are here. I think I have about an hour. Is the Queen here?"

"No, but I have seen Prince Ammed and his older brother enter as well as their entourage. There are not

many people from the Prince's country. I have seen only a handful and they look like bodyguards. There are many famous people here getting their picture taken with the young Prince and sitting on the groom's side of the church. He is very popular with the young stars. It's like a who's who of Hollywood is here today."

"Please get word to Que-tip to make sure the Fae keep an eye on the older brother. We need to know the second that he gets up to leave. Then we will know the bombs are ready to go off. If we have not heard from Charlie by then we will need to start a fire or something to evacuate the church in a hurry. While he's still sitting there, we are safe!"

"Okay, I am in the tunnel now. I will find the other entrance if there is one."

"Thank you Mick! You're great!"

Okay, now where to? I take a deep breath and close my eyes. Clear my mind and 'stop the constant chatter' as Mick taught. Breathe deep and let go. Breathe deep and let go.

I see a picture of being on the train and hear Florence telling me that the French are wary of people that smile too much.

Florence! That's it! The brochure says that Florence Nightingale is buried here. Where? I run along the hallway looking into all the rooms. *Why is this place so huge, I will never find it in time!* I run past one room after another. *What is that?*

I stop and back up. An old fashioned kerosene lamp is on top of a stone tomb. That must be her; she was known for visiting soldiers at night and was dubbed, 'The lady of the lamp'.

I wish I had a lamp right now. The room allocated to Florence Nightingale is dim, illuminated only by the low wattage lamp in the hall. Where is that door? *Yoo-hoo! Florence, are you here? I could use your help? Florence, come out, come out, wherever you are?*

Maybe it's a secret passage? I get on my knees and look under the tomb to check for loose stones and see a light. The light is in the shape of a beam given off by a pen light and coming closer. Dang those security guards, they would come here now. Maybe he will keep walking down the hallway and not come into this room. How do I talk my way out of this? Maybe he will keep making rounds and I can slip out?

I stay on my knees and the light comes into the room. *This is not good!* I can see the hand holding the light, the sleeve looks familiar. A bright red satin trimmed with gold braid on the cuff and exotic designs sewed into the fabric with gold thread. *The Prince!*

"Bridget, are you okay, where are you?"

"No Mick, I need help. I'm kneeling behind Florence Nightingale's tomb. This floor's cold. The Prince is here. He can't see me. I think he will be heading your way. He's walking to the end of the far wall. He's looking at a display from the Crimean War. Where the elaborate display ends, there's a wall, paneled in what looks like the original wood that built this place. He's raising his left hand and is putting it on a single panel above his head. With the other hand, he put the penlight in his mouth and* *is now pressing another panel at waist height. Great, it's opening! Can you see it from where you are?"*

"No, no movement at all."

"I don't think he's carrying anything. Could bombs be small enough to put in a pocket?"

"Get out of there now Bridget!"

"I will, I promise. Keep looking for him!"

"Of course, but you must promise me to leave the building now!"

"I will, I promise, don't you believe me?"

"I do, now get a move on!"

"Okay, bye, be careful, he may have a gun."

I will leave as soon as Prince Oama is in the passage. I plan to follow him, and leave the church as Mick demanded. I didn't lie to you Mick. I'm leaving the church the same way the Prince is.

We have to stop him. The panel is starting to close; I drop my shoes and run after him. Using both hands to keep it open, I step into a wooden structure that's creaking with my every move.

Interlude

They are coming your way

"Sam, they are coming your way. We are in luck, no Morrigan followers in sight. They must believe their job is done so they are off to find new people to corrupt."

"I got the one in front Alan, you take the guy following. David, be sure to keep his attention away from the trip wires. We want these blokes caught up tight as can be."

"Right On."

"Ladies, are you all set to make sure the guards are ready to get to work?"

"Sure thing Cade, Natalie and I have them covered."

"Thanks Leonda, how about you Lynne, are you still with Charlie?"

"I have him. I may have to turn off the computer to get his attention, but he will be there."

Chapter 21

The Prince is Armed

Thank goodness Prince Oama is making so much noise himself that he doesn't notice any additional noise. I let the door close behind me, and try not to cough on the dust and dirt that the Prince has stirred up. I hurry after him and his barely visible beam of light. If I lose him now I'll scream. I just don't want to think of what this dirt is doing to my new outfit. My nylons are toast. Ouch, what am I walking on... thank goodness I don't have a light. I really don't want to know.

My cell phone starts blasting the Star Spangled Banner, Mary's idea of a joke when she programmed my ring tone. I gasp aloud, jump and take a couple of steps to the wall. I immediately bite down on my lip as I hurry to shut it off. I get it out of my pocket and read a text from Charlie. "Terrorists and explosives in custody, call later." I'm so happy; I can't wait to tell Peter.

Then I hear it, deadly silence, no retreating footsteps, and there is no light. With the primitive instinct of the hunted, I know he is out there, waiting for me. He has heard my cell. I listen to the now silent room and cry out, *"Mick I'm in a room under the crypt. There must be a way out of here into the tunnel. I got word that we're not going to be blown up but Prince Oama knows that I followed him, and is now waiting for me. I'm trapped. If I move, and try to go back up to the crypt, he'll hear me. What should I do?"*

"Stay where you are I am coming to get you."

"Please don't, he has a gun!"

I feel my way forward, hoping to get to the darkest side of the room, away from any sudden light. I move, but not fast enough. The light hit my face.

"Who are you? Ah, the clumsy lady from the reception. Are you a reporter? No matter, there is nothing to report."

I scream, but it is the kind of scream I've had in my nightmares, a choked soundless cry that reaches no one. I turn to run and use my mind to create a shell around me for protection. Fear stifles my first attempt and before I can make another a lacerating pain sliced me in two. The force of the bullet knocks me to the ground. My heart is racing with fear and pain I yell out, *"I love you, Mick, I'm sorry, I messed up."*

I feel Mick materialize beside me and hear him say *"Stay with her."*

Moments later I hear a blood curdling scream that you'd hear in a nightmarish movie and open my eyes.

"Que-tip, where's Mick, is he okay?"

"He is fine now, how are you?"

"I think I may have passed out. I have an unfortunate tendency to freak myself out at the worst possible moment."

I look down at my beautiful new outfit covered in blood.

"I'm okay, if I don't look at the blood, my blood, yuck. I can do this, or pass out again, whichever comes first. Mick taught me to protect myself with a shell or heal myself whichever was needed. I will relax; okay breathe…okay not too deeply."

I feel lightheaded and woozy. I look at the wound and somehow knew the bullet had passed through and nothing vital was damaged. I have to stop the bleeding. I went to work with my mind to close the exit wound. I then concentrate on closing the entrance wound. With that done I give myself permission to pass out again.

Chapter 22

Back to Bed

I wake up, just where I want to be, at home in Battersea, in my own bed. I won't even question how I got clean and into my PJ's. I feel good, but boy do I have to use the bathroom. I open my eyes and see that I have a room full of visitors.

"Ahh, guys, can this wait a bit. I would like a little privacy for now."

No one moves. Finally Michele comes over, and without looking around says, "Peter, please take Mick into the front parlor, we will join you there soon."

I smile at a calm and efficient Michele. I think she thought of me, at this moment, like a puppy needing medical attention. She is acting so professional. A little strange, but as long as she helps me to the bathroom, I am fine with strange. If she had only seen what I saw when I opened my eyes, she would really freak out. My entire new family was crammed into this small bedroom: Que-tip, David, Alan, Cade, Deirdre, Regan, Kearin, Natalie, Ana, Kasondra, Samantha, Leonda, Tracy and a dozen other faeire.

Friar Xavier has also brought a friend I recognize. Florence, she's sitting on the bed, looking very concerned. A Nurse is a nurse forever I guess. I lean on both Michele and Florence as I make my way to the bathroom. This is really getting to be a pain. I've got to get good enough to not get injured. When I sit down, I still have no privacy. Michelle, puzzled, states the obvious!

"You have no fever now. Actually, your skin feels cool to the touch."

"I'm a fast healer."

Little did she know that leaning on a ghost would bring down anyone's fever. It's like being immersed in a bathtub filled with ice.

After a lot of fussing by both of my caregivers, I am allowed to sit up in the front parlor. Peter has made a pot of tea and brought more cupcakes. After the room came into focus I ask, "How are the dogs doing?"

"The Dorgis are all showing a little sign of being malnourished but there are no ill effects of the ether that the villains used to keep them quiet. I hope they keep those monsters in a kennel for life!"

"Hey, it's great to see your French attitude showing. I wouldn't want you angry at me. Good thing your 'villains' are safe behind bars."

We all laugh. It's great to see Peter happy. He's looking at Michelle with more than just laughter in those eyes. Hmm, another romance in the air, I've got to stop introducing my girl friends to guys.

"Peter did you fill Michelle in on what happened at the church?"

"Yes, I did. She thought that you were very brave to follow the Prince to get an autograph for her."

"You Americans are Hollywood crazy. Why would a crowd of people want an autograph from the Prince?

Imagine having a crowd of people knock you down a flight of stairs. All of that pushing and shoving for an autograph, crazy. He is in all the papers, you should see."

I quickly read the headlines:

The Times read. "Queen faces empty altar!"

The Sun read,. "Lady gets cold feet."

The Telegraph read. "Prince Oama pleads "No comment" on hurt feelings of younger brother."

"What! I thought Prince Oama would be in jail....oh no!"

I look over at Florence and remember our discussion on the train, *'Someone who smiles all the time is not to be trusted.'*

"You were not talking just about the French, were you?"

Florence gives me a slight smile and waves goodbye. I look around at Mick and all of the Fae gathered.

For Michelle's sake, I hold up the papers and pretend that I am reading and ask, *"It was Prince Ammed in the crypt?"*

Mick is unusually quiet and Que-tip answers, *"It was, it seems he had a brilliant plan to remove his brother from his rightful place next in line to the throne and place the blame on England. He would appear from the rubble as a survivor and begin to assist in the rescue mission. He had it all planned. Mick was able to read his thoughts when he met up with him in the tunnel."*

"Why isn't the real story in the papers?"

"Politics. Our government is honoring Prince Oama's request and Lady Chaternning's family is being paid quite handsomely to take the blame for backing out of the

wedding. The only knowledge the public will have of any of this is that the Lady left Prince Ammed waiting at the altar."

"Is Prince Ammed in jail in his own country?"

"Not exactly, it seems he had a bit of a fright. Something he saw in the tunnel has affected his mind. When Charlie found him, he was lying in the fetal position, babbling about fire breathing dragons.' He will be in a mental facility for the rest of his life."

"What about the guys that they caught with the explosives?"

"They are local hires, same as the guys they arrested for snatching the dogs. The Yard knows they were paid by an outside source but cannot trace the money back to the source. Both crimes will go on the books as solved and that makes the public happy."

"Who was behind the dog-napping?"

"We will never know for certain."

I look around the room.

"Thank you all so very much. Without your help, this would have been a major disaster."

David flies over to me and kneels on the paper. *"A thousand pardons my lady. We were not there to protect you. We have all been very anxious to hear that you have prevailed."*

"David, you were all doing what was asked of you. I have learned that I must discover my gifts myself. I could have prevented my injury, if I had kept calm as I was taught. This incident has shown me that I must be calm when I come up against Morrigan. For only with inner strength will I overcome all that she has in store for me."

I look at all the Fae gathered. *"I will be in touch soon, for I know now that I will soon face Morrigan, and will need you all by my side."*

They all twirl and amidst a rainbow of color, leave. The room suddenly looks dull and drab without all of that wonderful, sparkling color.

"Bridgette, you are very quiet. Are you feeling well?"

"I'm fine, Michelle, just tired. I think I'll go back to bed. I'm really not feeling any pain. Just a little stiff but mostly tired. I wonder if this is what fire fighters and law enforcement officer's face, extreme high shots of adrenalin and then the drop, the all over sense of exhaustion. I just need some sleep, don't worry."

I woke to daylight coming in the window. I hear excited voices and then realize that it is Michelle and Peter, *why are they here?* They are very happy about something. I get up, grab my old robe and open the door just in time to witness Peter and Michelle kiss. I was closing the door to give them some privacy, when I notice Mick with his paws over his eyes, and laugh out loud.

"Ah, *Oui*, you are awake. We have such news for you. Come sit with us."

"What's up with you guys, you look so happy."

Peter is waving a cream colored, heavily embossed envelope in the air. He waits until I sit and then hands me an invitation, "The Lord Chamberlain has been commanded by Her Majesty to invite you to the Investiture of Peter Cairns..."

"Wow fancy, what does this mean?"

"I don't know how to thank you Bridget. Charlie told the Queen that *I* was responsible for saving St. Paul's and *I am to be knighted.* It will only be an honorary Knighthood but I will be able to use *Sir Peter Cairns* on my business cards from now on," he bent his knee and gave a courtly bow that had us all laughing.

Peter sat down beside me and took my hand, he whispers, "You are not angry? You should be the one honored. You are the one that took all of the risks."

"Nonsense, you're the one that told me of the vision. You're the one responsible for saving the life of the Queen. Not me."

I'm embarrassed and know I'm starting to blush. Wanting to change the subject quickly, "Michelle, what are you reading?"

"The packet also contains all the information we require: dress codes, arrivals and departures, parking, etc."

"What are you going to do?"

"Good form dictates that one always accepts."

"I know that, of course you will. Write to her right away. That's so great. I'm so proud of you. Wow, my cousin will be an honorary Knight."

"You, Michelle and Charlie will be there to witness it."

"No way!"

"The form of an investiture has remained the same since 1910. Each recipient is entitled to invite three guests to accompany them on their special day."

"Did you tell Charlie?"

"Of course, I owe Charlie a great deal."

"Bridget, this is life changing. It will surely be a boost to my business. I may have so many paying clients that I will be able to afford to make a permanent change in my home life." The last he said looking lovingly at Michelle.

I look over at a blushing Michelle. "What will we wear?"

"I am reading the pages that came with the invitation. I am surprised to see how traditional life surrounding the British Court still is. No other institution could in this modern age still consider recommending that "women should wear hats" and advising that men wear "morning dress or uniform. White gloves are still the form, and I bet that they will stay immaculately clean as they glide along banisters, shake proffered royal hands, and wave goodbye in the ever-familiar royal manner."

"Well, I guess we don't have to worry about spreading germs."

"This is not a normal investiture. Those papers are for the traditional ceremonies. Charlie told me that we are invited to the ball that will be held in my honor, but not publically. The reason that will be given for the ball will be the birthday of a royal family member. Normally an investiture is a daytime affair. The Queen does not wish to announce anything that had to do with the plan to destroy the Cathedral."

"Peter..."

"Bridget I have told Michelle everything *about myself*. She is not concerned with my gift, does not think I am a freak."

"No, No, it is a special gift to help others. Not a bad thing. If it was not for your 'feelings' the Queen would be no longer."

"We are all going to a ball?"

"Yes, you will be escorted by Charlie and I will, of course, escort my Michelle."

"How will you be crowned?"

Peter laughed and it was great to see him so happy and carefree.

"Actually I will be dubbed, as I am sure that you have seen in the movies."

"They actually do that with a sword?"

"Yes"

"That is so cool."

"What do we do?"

"We will all arrive at The Palace an hour early. We will then be conducted to the State Ball Room where we will be rehearsed in the procedure for being presented to The Queen.

"Then we all stand when The Queen enters the Ball Room and we remain standing. The Lord Chamberlain then begins the ceremony proper by announcing the category of the honor. He then reads out my name and a brief explanation of why I have been honored.

"The only break from the form is that I will be the only recipient, rather than the customary much larger group. Only my guests and those in a position of security of the Queen and country will be present."

"So you kneel before The Queen and she says *"Arise Sir Knight......"*

"No, that is a complete fiction."

"Darn, most of the posh and circumstances will be missed."

"It will still be an experience we will never forget."

"Before I forget, Charlie wants you to call him as soon as you are feeling up to company. He would like to come to visit."

"First I really need a shower and something to eat, I'm starving."

Chapter 23

Where's Mick?

We continue talking while we ate Michelle's version of grilled cheese sandwiches. Who ever heard of them being made with white cheese? Don't know what kind it is, but it taste great.

I feel like a new person, clean, rested and my belly full. All is well with the world. I lean down to give Mick a bite of my sandwich but he isn't at his usual place next to me. He isn't even in the dining room.

"Hey Mick, are you hungry, do you want a bite of my sandwich?"

No answer.

"Hey guys, did you see Mick?"

"I let him out back when I was making the sandwiches. Don't worry. I left the back door open. He will come in when he is ready. He may be just lazing around in the sun."

Maybe now that the crisis is over Mick went back to his real home. I guess he only likes to hang around when I need him. I push the sandwich away and announce that I am going for a walk.

After listening to their arguments for what seems like forever, I open the front door.

"Hurry back, we have to practice making our obeisance."

"I'll be back soon."

Wonder what the heck obeisance is, maybe purple cheese sandwiches. I check the back yard again before I leave. As I suspect, it's empty. No Mick.

I only walk a block when I hear, *"Why so glum, chum?"*

"Hi Que-tip, I thought you were off playing with your mates?"

"I did that, everyone's resting now."

We walk along in silence. I'm happy she isn't bugging me with questions. I have no answers just major questions of my own, like what the heck do I do now?

My latest nightmares have me out in a cold, windy day. Maybe I get to goof off until fall. Would Morrigan give me a couple of months to get a plan in place? I doubt it, but I just don't know.

I need Mick; he's the one I like to bounce off ideas with. I'll give him some free time. He must be very tired teaching me. I hope he isn't mad at me. I did leave the Cathedral, just not the way he thought I would. Funny how much I miss him when he is not around. The rest of my friends and family are just not the same. When he's near, I feel safe, no, not just safe. I feel like I am someone special. With people, I always feel as if I am not good enough. That whatever I do will not measure up. With Mick, I feel as if I am accepted, just as I am, with all of my faults. He will be back soon. He wouldn't leave me now, would he?

I open the front door to a madhouse. Charlie has arrived and is talking with Peter and Michelle as to what to expect at the Palace. There are a dozen or so faeire ladies fluttering about. They are so excited that the small front parlor looks like a rainbow erupted.

Tired from my walk, I try to slip in quietly and head to the peace and quiet of my room.

"Brigitte, I am so happy you are here. We must practice our obeisance."

"Our what?"

"Our obeisance, it is most simple. It involves a curtsey to the Queen."

I almost pack my bags and head home.

"Back home we don't even curtsey to the First Lady. Can I just nod?"

"Men are blessed with having only to bow, a most simple act. A correct bow involves only a deep nod," Charlie informs us.

"Out of respect it is expected for ladies to curtsey. If that is not comfortable, since you are not English citizens, we will understand," sighs Peter.

How can he put so much guilt into a sigh?

"Can I just bow from the waist?"

"Bridgette it is so easy. You and I will practice this obeisance. We will do it. We will do it for you Peter, and for the fact that we respect your Queen."

Okay, I'm stuck now, just great. Charlie, who had already received an honour for his help in locating the missing dogs, continues his instructions.

"Once you have been presented, you are faced with the question of what to say. The Queen is always addressed as "Your Majesty" on the first count and thereafter as "Ma'am"; this should rhyme with jam, not palm. Other members of the royal family are treated with similar respect: "Your Royal Highness" then "Sir" or "Ma'am.

"You should let the royal personage lead the conversation, not try to change the subject, and ask only the politest of questions."

"Is Your Majesty enjoying the performance?" is acceptable, but "How's Philip and Charles?" is most definitely, absolutely out of the question. When you are in conversation with a member of the royal family, be yourself but remember that Her Royal Highness is not going to appreciate your company if it is too loud, tongue-tied, rude, or bumptious."

I'm sure he was looking at me when he said that. What the heck is bumptious anyway? I know, I can play, 'I'm not feeling too good card'. I will just play sick and not go.

I look at the excited faeire and say to my human company, "Excuse me guys. I'm a little worn out from my walk. I'll take a quick nap and join you guys later for dinner. Will that be okay?"

"Pardon, Brigitte. We are thoughtless. We will speak quietly. You rest and don't worry about dinner. We will get take out and wake you later on, when it is all set."

"You are not going to chicken out, Bridget. We are here to help you."

"Thank you Que-tip, ladies. All I can think of is the movies I watched where lines of young women parade before the Queen like vestal virgins adorned in white with feathers, trains, and fans to make their deep, reverential, and well-practiced curtseys. I will look like a fool, and I have nothing to wear."

With that Regan, Natalie, Kasondra and Kearin open the large wooden wardrobe that I use for my closet. I can't believe my eyes.

"Where did all of this come from?"

I flop down on my bed in shock. Tracey and Ana fly over to the closet, and with the help of several others; they begin to bring me the treasures. First is a shawl made of the finest Irish lace imaginable. I've seen a picture of this kind of handmade lace in the historical society achieves housed near the Book of Kells, but I didn't believe any still existed.

The parade continues with, beige leather heels, which feel like smooth butter, silk nylons, and long gloves that button at my wrist and go to my elbow, a silk slip, strapless bra and underwear, so delicate to be almost invisible.

Then the most beautiful evening gown I have ever seen in my life. Even in Vogue. The strapless top is a deep burgundy maroon embedded in a hundred places with pink Austrian Crystals. The skirt is a heavenly mixture of colors ranging from a light pink to a deep burgundy and everything in between.

"This is impossible. It's not mine? Whose is it?"

"It is a gift, My Lady."

"Who from, is it Geraldine....?"

I stop speaking and gawk as I spot Mick; he has materialized next to me on the bed. In his mouth he holds a black velvet jewelry box.

"For me?"

Mick leans over and drops the box in my lap. I just stare at it. I've received a few presents over the years from Mary and her Mom but this is way different than a Nike shirt.

"Please open it."

My hands shake as I open it. The feel of the velvet box with the deep silver etchings is so wonderful, it took me awhile. I open what looks like a box of faeire magic. There's a rainbow of color coming from one beautiful stone on a sterling silver chain. The stone is the size of a fifty cent piece and it's held in place by an intricately designed silver surround. I lean over to get next to the light and look closer at the design. I see a ring of faeire etched in silver. Cut so perfectly, I could tell who modeled for the piece. They are all there; Que-tip aka RaeAnne, Regan, Kearin, Natalie, Cade, David, Ana, Kasondra, Alan, Deirdre, and the others that so bravely helped me succeed in this challenge.

"This is beautiful; I can't believe it's real. What kind of stone is this?"

"It is an Alexandrite stone."

"Look in the box, there are earrings to match!"

"There is a bracelet as well!"

I move more pink tissue and uncover a beautiful set of stud earrings and a bracelet of matching Alexandrite stones.

"This is way too much!"

"Please do not insult the giver by not accepting. It is a way of saying that you are loved."

I can't help it. I cry.

"I can't believe my Great's did this, isn't it wonderful?"

I grab Mick, hug him, and cry so hard that I start hiccupping. The more I hiccup the more the faeire laugh. Soon they have me laughing and dancing around the room with them. After a few minutes, I again flop down on the bed. I repress a yawn.

"We will leave you now to rest. Is it okay to come back later? We would love to watch you practice your curtsey," giggles Kearin.

I kick off my shoes and lay down on the bed. Close my eyes, and feel movement. I open them to watch Mick cover me with a light throw. "Mick," I open my arms, he lies next to me with his head on my shoulder.

"I was so worried; I thought you wouldn't come back. I thought that you were mad at me for not really listening to you. I'm so sorry Mick. I had to stop him. I couldn't let him blow up the Queen."

"I know my girl, I was angry but not with you but myself. I was not there to prevent you from getting hurt."

"I guess this is the way I am destined to learn my lessons. When I thought I was going to die, all I could think of was you. I love you Mick. I know that my greats are making you stay with me and teach me the lessons that I need to learn. But do you think that you would like to come live with me? I think you would love it in the city. There is so much to do and they now have doggie parks and we could go walking in Central Park. I know wherever you are, I would be safe."

There is no answer. I hug Mick tighter and try to keep the tears from my eyes.

"I'm sorry, Mick, silly question. I've a job to do first. You think about it, and when I stop Morrigan we can talk about it again. Okay? Morrigan needs to stop trying to see how far she can push people before they crack. I know she loves to see humans display our basest emotions-jealousy, greed, fear and hatred. She has the faeire working on that, but she can't want an all out war. Can she?"

"The deeper people sink into fear, the harder it is for them to reason. There is no telling how far Morrigan will push the human race. Her evil faeire are everywhere, affecting millions with fear and doubt, taking from them their hopes and dreams of a bright future."

I shiver. Mick licks my hand and snuggles closer. Blocking my thoughts as Mick has taught me, I soon fall asleep.

After a great take-out Indian dinner, Michelle and I practice in front of the floor length mirror that the guys moved into the front parlor. I have never laughed so hard in my life. Whenever I stop laughing all I have to do is to look at the faeire gathered, or see the two straight-laced English gentlemen try to contain their laughter, and I burst out laughing again.

The curtsey is a difficult maneuver to execute; if it goes right it looks excellent as you descend towards the ground while shaking hands with The Queen, but if it goes wrong I can end up falling over and making a fool of myself, and ruining this event for everyone. Peter told me that I could just nod my head, but heck, I respect this powerful lady. If a little thing like a curtsey is a way to show that respect, than I will do it, or die trying.

Interlude

She is in love with a dog!

Mick watches the dark clouds as they gather over the sea. The darkness of the sky well matches his mood. The sky and sea are gathering strength to hit the small tower ledge he sat upon. Rain soaks his clothing; wind slashes his hair against his face.

Padraig materializes next to Mick.

"We watched what was happening. She did it again. Our girl used her ability to close the wound, and begin the healing process. She is growing stronger in her abilities and belief in herself as a warrior."

"That she is. She is accepting her gifts, and is comfortable in the world of Fae. My concern is that she does not yet believe that she is an equal to other humans."

"How could that be, she is more skilled than many others. There is only a handful that can close a wound, that can use the power of deduction and true faith to follow the signs they have been given, to move forward…," Padraig sputters.

"We should have come into her life earlier. The challenges of her birth have left their scars. It will take time for her to overcome them. She is a special woman but she does not yet know that."

"Will humans honor her good works?"

"Her cousin will be honored at the palace by the queen for his part in saving the dogs, and the cathedral."

"You sound angry that she is not being recognized by humans, as one that is special."

"She is very special," Mick said as he threw a rock far out into the Irish Sea.

Padraig looks at Mick for several seconds. "You are in love with her?"

"I am, there is nothing I can do, is there?"

"Not at present, please be patient. Do you know what her feelings are?"

"She has said she loves me."

"Then that is great news!"

Mick turns to his friend, and with pain reflected in his eyes, defies his friend to laugh.

"She is in love with a dog!"

Chapter 24

Buckingham Palace

This is surreal. I know those guards are going to come over here and kick me out. I don't belong here.

Charlie reaches into the limo that has been hired for the evening. With one hand holding the skirt of my gown in place, I swing my legs out of the car and stand. I hold onto his hand for dear life. I know he senses my nervousness for he put his arm through mine and with his support I somehow manage to walk past the Royal Guards and into the grand hallway.

I thought that the State Room where we were schooled in what to expect was overwhelming. It is nothing compared to this. Two sconces are holding several lights shaped like candles. They help to highlight the gold bronze balustrade. The transition from the comparative darkness of the Grand Hall to the brightness of the Grand Staircase is amazing. I have to tell my feet to keep moving and not just stand there and gawk.

Peter is continuing his role of guide, acting as if he is not as nervous as we are.

"The stairs are lit by a shallow dome of etched glass. Queen Victoria requested that the series of portraits of her immediate family were displayed around the upper part of the stairs. These include her grandparents and her parents. Thus the portraits serve as a kind of 'receiving line' so that whoever climbs the staircase is simultaneously received by her family."

The Investiture in the Ballroom went by in a blur. At one time the Queen came over to me and said something I didn't fully understand. I can't wait to speak with Mick so that he can explain. The Queen leaves the ballroom and we are left standing with a dozen or so members of her 'inner circle'.

Within a few minutes the ballroom begins to fill up with various family members. Peter is like a little kid in a candy store. He and Charlie are telling us who it is that we are looking at. I nod to one guy that looks to be part of a large party of folks who just arrived. He looks somewhat familiar.

"Charlie, who's that?"

"That guy belongs to the Knights of the Garter, and the Royal Knights. He is speaking with Princess Alexandra, the Hon. Lady Ogilvy, The Duke of Kent, The Duke of Gloucester, The Duke of York, The Princess Royal, and The Prince of Wales..."

A fanfare sounds, and The Sovereign, accompanied by Prince Philip, Duke of Edinburgh, makes his progress to her table, as if this is the Queen's first appearance in the ballroom today. I am happy to see Friar Xavier walk solemnly behind the family. He looks like royalty himself, until he sees me and dances up to the beautiful decorated ceiling.

"I can't believe that we are this close to the Royal family," I whisper to Michelle, who just nods. She is still speechless from having the Queen acknowledge her at

Peter's investiture, and thank her for her *continued* care of her canine family.

"Would you care to dance?"

I smile at Charlie. He looks so handsome in his formal tux.

"I would love to."

Michelle and Peter join us on the dance floor, they look so happy together.

"Thank you for your help, Charlie, this is a dream that I don't want to end. Hope it all doesn't disappear at midnight."

"If it does, I promise to find your glass slipper and return it to you. I am a detective you know."

We laugh and twirl around the room. Charlie tells me that I'm dancing the waltz. Wow, wait till I tell Mary. She will bust a seam laughing. Wish I could've reached her by phone, but she and Simon are now in parts of Scotland that don't get cell coverage.

I look around the room, suddenly feeling as if someone is watching me. No not just watching me, something else, some strong feeling, but not evil.

"That guy over there by the column is staring at us. I asked you his name earlier but you rattled off so many names I don't remember his. Why do you think he's staring?"

"That is Lord Howth. He stares at every beautiful woman. Would you like to meet him?"

"Wait I..."

Charlie has me by the hand, and we walk across the dance floor to meet a Lord. Nothing like being a little obvious is there.

"Hi Michael, how are you? I thought you were still at your summer home?"

"Good Evening Charles, a little business to do in town. I will be heading back up North soon."

"May I introduce you to a good friend of mine? Bridget, this is Lord Howth."

"How do you do Lord Howth. I hope I'm not supposed to curtsey. I accomplished that once today, and hope never to have to do it again." He laughs and I see the most beautiful brown eyes that I've ever seen. They are more like amber, shinning with life, and yet his smile can't hide a tinge of sadness. I wonder what could make this gorgeous hunk of manhood sad. He says something about calling him Michael and laughs some more. All traces of sadness gone. Did I imagine it?

"Charlie may I ask your lady for a dance?" Charlie nods.

"I would love to dance, thank you," Bridget says.

Lord Howth and I dance the next three dances. We talk when we can, but I can't remember what we said. I just know that I feel like I'm floating.

"I can't get over the feeling that I know you."

"Would you like to walk out on the terrace for a bit of air?"

"I would love to." I notice as we pass the other women in the room, no matter what age, are all trying to get his attention. He's charming. Maybe he is a little too good looking, too charming. Probably he's a spoiled rich kid. Not my type at all.

I look back to where Charlie is sitting by himself, "I'm sorry Michael. I'm a horrible date. Charlie is all alone. Please take me back to our table."

"Of course, right away. Are you in love with my friend Charlie?"

"That's none of your business. We're friends, and I don't intentionally neglect my friends."

At the table Lord Howth apologizes to Charlie.

"Sorry old chap, don't know what came over me. It must have been the lobster."

He turns to me, and winks. His eyes are like warm honey. He holds my hand. With a slight nod of his head he brings my hand to his lips and at the last minute, turns my wrist to the area not covered in material and kisses it. I just stand there in shock watching him. He looks into my eyes and smiles.

Luckily I'm standing by my chair otherwise I would have fallen down. Talk about a 100 watt smile. What a hottie. I can still feel the burn from those lips on my skin.

"What was that he said about a lobster?" asks an amused Charlie.

"Lobster?" I look after Lord Howth as he leaves the hall.

"Oh no, he's the guy who helped me up at the reception. I was wearing a lobster on my head."

The rest of the night is a blur.

When I get home I'm so wired I just know I couldn't possibly get to sleep, but I'm in a deep slumber as soon as my head hits the pillow.

"Mick, Mick... Help me, Mick!"

"I am here Bridget, wake up now. I am with you. I am here."

I wake up, and hold onto Mick. The nightmare was bad this time.

"Do you want to talk about it?"

"It's the same nightmare I've been having for the past year. I'm running. People are screaming and crying. There is fire and this unholy whispering. I can't explain it. I don't know what she says. It's in a language I can't recognize."

"What made this more frightening than the others?"

"The whispering is no longer from far away. I can feel her breath on me. I will meet up with her soon. I've got to get ready. I'm scared, Mick."

"You are ready Bridget. It has been foretold that you will meet Morrigan. I will make sure that you will not meet her until you are ready to do battle, and win! I know of a place in Scotland where we will train. You will be safe there. We will succeed."

"Then why am I so scared?"

THE END?

Turn the page for a preview of Book Three, final book in the Brooklyn Leprechaun mystery series.

The final book of.
'The Brooklyn Leprechaun'
mystery series.

Magical Scotland

"Okay, I give up; it's getting late, I'll go back to the village and ask for better directions. Why did I trust a talking dog anyway?"

Magical Scotland

I turn to climb back down the hill, stop and stare. My little rental with the annoying GPS is now parked on a drive in the middle of a forest. Rising above the tallest trees I've ever seen is the top of a Castle.

Never one with a loss for words, my jaw drops open and I'm speechless.

The Castle towers several stories above a large, high-walled garden. It's probably built of pale stone, but sunset's fire turned it gold and gilded the roofs and chimneys. The same magic washes over the surrounding evergreens.

Green, yellow, pink and purple flags fly in the breeze. Watchtowers are at each corner manned by sentries. The walls must be at least 12 feet high. The garden or commons area between the wall and the castle itself must be a mile wide and a dozen miles long.

What on earth? Where did this all come from?
Wait a minute. Am I really questioning what I'm seeing? I've met my ancestors, '*The Great's*' the Queen of the Fae, the King of the Leprechaun, and I'm being tutored by a talking dog, so what's a castle appearing where there once were only rocks. No big deal. As my Aunt Molly would say, It tis a fine place to learn magic.

Made in the USA
Charleston, SC
17 January 2013